A diabolical scheme . . .

Eve stood in a pool of harsh light in front of Garner Rexton's desk. Garner himself, sitting in his desk chair, was hidden in the shadows.

"Stunts won't leave Team Fastex," Eve explained to her boss. "He's too loyal."

Garner leaned forward so that his face caught the light. "We had an agreement," he told her. "If Carlos Rey leaves Fastex, your debt to me is forgiven. And if he doesn't—"

A worried expression crossed Eve's pretty face.

Garner smiled, enjoying her discomfort. "Do I need to remind you that you owe me more money than you can ever possibly repay?" he asked.

"He would've quit, Mr. Rexton," Eve said quickly. "If Jack Fassler hadn't agreed to this team jump—"

"Wait," Garner said, interrupting her. He rubbed his chin, lost in thought. "All four Team Fastex drivers in a dangerous stunt jump . . ."

Eve watched anxiously as Garner swiveled his chair to the side and stared into the darkness. For a moment he seemed to vanish into the silent shadows.

"Fastex could lose four drivers instead of one . . ." Garner said slowly, thinking aloud. "If something tragic should happen, that is."

Collect all these awesome NASCAR Racers books!

NASCAR Racers: *How They Work*

NASCAR Racers: *Official Owner's Manual*

NASCAR Racers #1: *The Fast Lane*

NASCAR Racers #2: *Taking the Lead*

NASCAR Racers #3: *Tundra 2000*

NASCAR Racers #4: *Daredevil*

AND COMING SOON

NASCAR Racers: *Motorsphere to the Max*

NASCAR Racers: *Lightning Pace*

ATTENTION: ORGANIZATIONS AND CORPORATIONS

HarperEntertainment books may be purchased for educational, business, or sales promotional use. For information please write: Special Markets Department, HarperCollins Publishers Inc., 10 East 53rd Street, New York, NY 10022-5299.

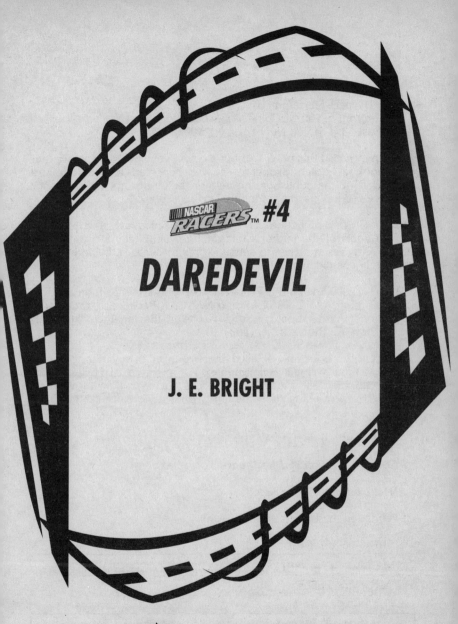

NASCAR RACERS™ #4

DAREDEVIL

J. E. BRIGHT

HarperEntertainment
An Imprint of HarperCollinsPublishers

HarperEntertainment
An Imprint of HarperCollins*Publishers*
10 East 53rd Street, New York, NY 10022-5299

First printing: September 2000

Cover illustration by Mel Grant

Designed by Jeanette Jacobs

Printed in the United States of America

ISBN 0-06-107191-9

Visit HarperEntertainment on the World Wide Web at
www.harpercollins.com

10 9 8 7 6 5 4 3 2 1

It was race day at Rexcor Raceway. The stands in the dark, sinister-looking stadium were teeming with happy, excited crowds all cheering for their favorite teams and drivers. The hooting and hollering was nearly deafening—but the noise of the crowd was nothing compared to the body-shaking rumble of the incredibly high-tech NASCAR Unlimited Series cars on the track.

Vvvvrrrrrrrrrroooooooooooommmmmmmmm!

A squadron of Unlimited Series cars zoomed around a sharp turn and gushed down a straight-away. Leading the line was Hondo Hines, a Team

Rexcor driver also known as Specter, and Team Fastex driver Stunts, officially Carlos Rey.

Stunts steered his car, trying to spurt past Specter. But whether Stunts shifted high or low on the track, Specter moved to block him.

"Hey, slow-poco!" Stunts hollered at Specter over the car's radio. "Get outta the way! This race is mine!"

Specter's only reply was a low, threatening laugh.

Up ahead of Stunts was Rexcor Raceway's world-famous loop-the-loop, an insanely dangerous stretch of track that arched hundreds of feet into the air.

Stunts gunned his engine and followed Specter into the loop-the-loop. The two cars zoomed up the steep ramp, and the crowd cheered wildly as the cars hurtled along the track upside down, high above the stadium. Specter and Stunts surged out the other side, with Specter still in the lead, and headed for a high-banked turn.

Both cars took the turn at unbelievable speed. Specter, followed closely by Stunts, cruised out of the turn and onto a long straightaway.

Specter activated his radio. "Junker, shed some parts," he commanded his Rexcor teammate. Junker's real name was Diesel Spitz. "I want metal on the track," Specter said grimly.

Across the infield, on the other side of the track, Junker's more than usually battered car roared

down a different straightaway. Junker smiled. *"Ja, you are wanting metal,"* he told Specter over the radio, "you are getting metal!"

Approaching Junker was Mark McCutchen, the Team Fastex driver better known as Charger. Junker veered and—

Crrrrrraaaannnnnngggg! He smashed into Charger. The sound was hideous.

Fighting to keep control, Charger managed to squeak by Junker mostly undamaged, but body panels fell off Junker's car and onto the track.

Meanwhile, Specter and Stunts were dashing toward the electronic flag board. The two drivers, almost side by side, roared under the flag board just as the yellow caution flag flashed on it. Specter banged Stunts's car sideways.

Crrrrrruunnnnnch!

Stunts was sent sliding, his tires squealing. Both tires on one side of Stunts's car blew out as he bumped over the sharp metal panels from Junker's car.

Stunts struggled with the steering wheel. "Good thing these cars got four wheels!" he cried. He reached for the lever on his dash that controlled his maneuvering jets.

Ffoooooooooooommmmm!

As soon as he pulled the lever, a powerful blast of flame exploded out of one of Stunts's jets. His car tilted up onto two wheels—and kept running.

3

An emergency helicopter hovered above the race-track. It dangled a huge magnet to pick up the chunks of metal that had been knocked off Junker's car. In a few seconds, the helicopter had cleaned up the garbage.

Douglas "Duck" Dunaka, the Team Fastex crew chief, stood aboard the Fastex IMP. The IMP—or Independently Mobile Pit unit—was a high-tech garage on wheels. During an off-track race, it was driven onto a road and used as a rolling pit stop. But most of the time it was parked in the pits and the racers drove up onto it for repairs or refueling as if it were an automotive aircraft carrier.

Duck raised a handheld radio to his mouth. "Stunts, pit for a tire change!" he ordered.

Stunts breezed along on two wheels. "And let Team Rexcor pass me?" he replied to Duck. "No way, man!"

"Drive smart, Carlos!" Duck called over the radio. "Third or fourth place is worth a lot of championship points. If you wreck, you could lose everything."

"It's all or nothing with me, Duck!" Stunts answered.

The electronic board flashed the green flag—all clear—as Specter blazed under it, followed by Stunts on two wheels.

Once again, Specter plunged through the loop-the-loop. Stunts took a deep breath, still up on two

4

wheels, as he chased Specter into the swooping track.

Amazingly, Stunts whizzed through the loop-the-loop on two wheels and then followed Specter down the long straightaway.

Zorina—another bad-tempered Team Rexcor driver, who used to be a fashion model—accelerated until she was hot on Stunts's tilted bumper.

The three cars blasted into the high-banked turn at the end of the straightaway and sizzled out onto another long stretch of flat track.

Specter swerved toward Stunts's car.

Still on two wheels, Stunts jerked the steering wheel hard to one side. He slipped into a controlled spin, his two wheels squealing. Stunts narrowly avoided hitting Specter's car.

But Specter crunched into Zorina as she was trying to pass Stunts on the other side. Her car heaved into the wall.

Kaaa-rraaaaaaashhhh!

Stunts grinned. Ahead of him, there was nothing but the finish line.

2

*T*he crowd went berserk as Stunts's car recovered from the spin and lurched across the finish line . . . just seconds ahead of Specter.

Suddenly the scene blurred, then went black.

The videotape had ended.

The big-screen TV that had played the tape was hanging over a counter in a diner—a hangout for race car drivers and bikers. Stunts and two good-looking girls sat at a table nearby. "Hey, hombre!" Stunts called to the diner's manager. "Run the tape again! There's nothing I like better than watching myself win!"

The girls with Stunts laughed appreciatively.

The manager had been wiping down the counter with a wet rag. He shrugged, unimpressed, as he picked up a remote. He pushed a button, and the tape restarted.

Stunts and the two girls watched the cars line up to start the race.

Vvvrrrrrrrooooooooommmmmmmmmmmm!

The deafening roar of an engine filled the diner.

Stunts called out to the manager again. "Hey—turn it down! I like to hear myself talk, too!"

Vvvrrrrrrrooooooooommmmmmmmmmmm!

A motorcycle rumbled into the diner. The cycle was making the roar—not the cars on TV. The motorcycle screeched to a stop beside Stunts's table.

Surprised that a motorcycle had buzzed right through the front door of the diner, Stunts tried not to show his shock. Instead, he studied the driver. A helmet hid the biker's identity.

"If you're looking for a place to park," Stunts said, "try the lot outside."

The rider pulled off the helmet, revealing a beautiful face and long blond hair.

Stunts recognized her instantly—and couldn't believe his eyes. She was a famous stunt driver, a female Evel Knievel. "You're Eve Kildare!" Stunts yelped.

7

"And you're Carlos Rey," Eve shot back. "You ran a pretty good race today—but you aren't good enough to catch me." Eve slipped her helmet back on. Then she revved her engine and burst out of the diner on her motorcycle.

Stunts stood up and rushed to follow Eve.

"We're as pretty as she is!" one of the groupies at the table protested.

Stunts paused and glanced back. "That's true, *chica*," he told her. "But Eve's a better driver." He hustled out of the diner.

After jumping on his motorcycle, Stunts revved the engine to life. He slipped on his helmet and blasted off after Eve.

Eve cruised down a dark forested road near the diner that was often used for casual competition. Stunts wasn't far behind, leaning into the familiar turns, his motorcycle engine roaring. He caught sight of the red taillight of Eve's motorcycle up ahead, flashing in the darkness. Stunts grinned—he was gaining on her.

Up the road through the forest was a deep, dark quarry.

Eve roared toward it, sliding into a turn and onto a road leading to the quarry. Stunts zoomed after her, slipping a little through the turn. He pursued Eve down the quarry road.

The quarry, abandoned by miners years ago, had steep stone walls a hundred feet high. The tops of

the walls were covered by thick trees and plants, and far below, a wide lake shimmered in the moon-light. A few flat boulders broke the lake's calm surface.

Suddenly, Eve gunned her engine and cruised up a portable ramp she'd set up at the quarry's edge. She flew over the quarry, sailing through the air.

On the other side, Eve's rear tire just cleared the edge, spraying gravel into the lake far below. But she'd made it!

Stunts's mouth dropped open when he saw the ramp ahead of him in the road. "Whoa—no!" he hollered.

He rushed up the ramp and flew off the edge, soaring over the quarry. But Stunts tumbled off his motorcycle in midair. He fell toward the water and the jagged rocks beneath him.

"No!" he cried.

3

*S*ploosh!

Stunts and his motorcycle smacked into the water, making waves in the serene moonlit lake.

Eve rode her motorcycle slowly down an access road leading toward the water. She didn't seem worried about Stunts at all.

Stunts popped up in the lake, unhurt. He shook his head to clear it, then swam for the bank where the quarry access road met the water.

Sitting astride her motorcycle, Eve waited for him on the shore. She unbuckled her helmet and pulled it off.

When Stunts reached the shallow part of the lake, he stopped. He stood chest-deep in the water as he looked up at Eve. In the moonlight, she was stunningly beautiful—a motorcycle mama fantasy come to life.

Eve smirked at him. "You swim almost as good as you drive," she teased Stunts.

"I would've made that jump," Stunts shot back, "if I'd known it was coming."

"I know you would've," Eve replied evenly.

Stunts stared at her in total shock. He hadn't expected her to *compliment* him!

Eve met his stare calmly. For a few seconds, they just watched each other. Finally, Eve took a deep breath. "That's why I want you to join my act," she said. "As my partner."

Stunts gaped at her, splashing a little in the cold water. He didn't know how to respond to her offer. It was tempting, but . . .

Before Stunts could say no, Eve rushed on. "You'll make more money than you ever could driving for Team Fastex—and you'll be more famous."

"I can't quit Team Fastex," Stunts said slowly. Then he smiled. "But that doesn't mean I can't do a little moonlighting *between* races."

He waded to the edge of the water. "Part-time partners," Stunts said, extending his hand. "Have we got a deal?"

Eve reached down and shook his hand. "Deal."

With a hard yank, Stunts pulled her into the water. *Splash!*

Eve yelped as she toppled into the lake. Seconds later, she struggled to the surface beside Stunts. Standing up, shoulder-deep in the water, Eve gasped and spluttered, soaking wet.

Stunts grinned at her, and they collapsed in laughter.

The desert canyon was hundreds of feet deep. Its jagged orange rock walls glinted in the harsh sunlight. Clouds drifted through the canyon's depths, often obscuring the slim trickle of a blue river down below. On both sides of the canyon, long metal ramps had been set up.

Vrrrrrrrrrooooooooommmmmmmm!

On the near side of the canyon, Stunts revved the engine of an Unlimited Series car. It wasn't his—the car was painted in fiery colors with Eve's and Stunts's names printed on the doors. A few days had passed since they'd made their part-time partnership deal, and their plan was right on track.

Wearing her helmet, Eve buzzed up to Stunts on a special stunt motorcycle equipped with rocket boosters. She skidded to a stop beside the car.

"Ready, Carlos?" Eve asked him through the window.

"This really is an Unlimited Series car," Stunts

said, shaking his head in disbelief. "Where did you get it?"

Perched on her motorcycle, Eve shrugged. "I've got a financial backer with deep pockets," she said. "Let me worry about business. You just worry about this jump!"

Stunts pointed out his car window at the writing on the door. "And why is your name above mine?" he asked.

Eve raised her eyebrows. "Because this stunt was my idea," she replied coolly. "Got a problem with that?" Without waiting for a reply, Eve roared off.

Tires squealing, Stunts charged after her, racing for the ramp.

The motorcycle and the car launched up the ramp side by side. Hundreds of feet below their vehicles, the desert canyon gaped and the thin winding river sparkled in the sunlight.

Remote control TV cameras mounted on poles near the ramp swiveled to follow Eve and Stunts. A crowd cheered from a temporary grandstand set up on the other side of the canyon, near the faraway ramp.

Eve and Stunts blasted off the ramp, with Eve's rocket boosters firing. As they left solid ground behind them, Stunts fired his maneuvering jets. Then he swooped into a barrel roll around Eve in midair!

On the other side of the canyon, the motorcycle

and the car landed on the ramp with a loud *thunk*. They slid to a stop in front of the grandstand.

As soon as the dust settled, Eve hopped off her bike, and Stunts jumped out of his racer. They held up their arms triumphantly as they bowed to the screaming crowd.

Eve nudged Stunts's arm. "That barrel roll wasn't part of the plan!" she muttered angrily. "That stunt was dangerous enough without your tricks!"

Stunts grinned. In a cool, confident voice, he said, "Next time I get my name first."

4

*B*ig River Raceway *gleamed in the* morning sunlight. The giant glass globe of the Motordome loomed above the brand-new track like an alien spacecraft. The stands were empty, and a faint echo resounded through the stadium. For Team Fastex, it was only a practice day.

Vrrrrrrrrrooooommmm!

Stunts's car flung out of a turn at the end of a straightaway. His tires were barely whirling blurs as he shredded down the gleaming track.

Duck stood aboard the Team Fastex IMP, carefully watching Stunts's progress. He could tell immediately that Stunts was not performing up to his ability. Glancing at his stopwatch Duck shook his head in disgust.

As Stunts finished another lap, Duck contacted him over the radio. "Bring her in," Duck ordered.

Stunts's car breezed into pit row and drove up onto the IMP.

Grimacing, Duck swung up alongside Stunts in the hydraulic mechanic's seat. "You gotta get your head back into your driving," he scolded Stunts. "Your lap times are way off."

"Guess I'm just not with it today," Stunts said.

Duck sniffed and crossed his arms. "Maybe that stunt jump I saw on TV took something outta you."

Stunts narrowed his eyes and glared at Duck. "What I do on my own time is my own business," he said. Then he slammed his car into reverse and backed down off the IMP.

Stunts's car whipped down pit row and pulled onto the track for a few more practice laps.

This time there were twice as many fans crowding the grandstand as there had been for the canyon stunt. And the crowd was twice as loud, psyched up to see Eve and Stunts's cool car-and-motorcycle tricks in person. Collapsible metal bleachers were set up along an old rented raceway, and stunt ramps were in position on the patchy grass of the infield.

Vrroooooooommmmmmmmmm!

Stunts revved the purring engine of Eve's mysterious Unlimited Series car. This time, Stunts was pleased to see his name appear before Eve's.

Out his window, Stunts waved to the roaring crowd. In the cheering mass of people, he could see signs that read, WE LOVE YOU STUNTS and ROCK AND ROLL, EVE! Stunts grinned as he gunned the car around the track. He thrived on this kind of attention and admiration. Nothing was better than fame. *Nothing.*

Eve waited on her motorcycle at the opposite end of the track. She was directly in front of the grandstand. With a wave to the cheering crowd, Eve burst into motion, steering her motorcycle toward Stunts.

They roared toward the ramps in the infield from opposite directions. Eve's bike and Stunts's car surged up the jump ramps and sailed into the sky. Only inches apart, they nearly touched in midair.

When Stunts's car landed, he immediately dashed up a looping ramp that thrust him into the air—back the way he'd just come. But this time his car was upside down.

After holding his upside-down position long enough for the crowd to get a good look, Stunts fired his maneuvering jets to swing the car upright again.

The car landed smoothly. Stunts screeched to a

stop beside Eve, who was pulling off her helmet and shaking out her hair.

Even before the car had come to a complete halt, Stunts scrambled out of his window and pulled off his helmet. Then he wrapped his arms around Eve. And kissed her.

The crowd went mad with cheers, screams, and wild applause.

After the kiss, Eve stepped back from Stunts, staring at him in surprise. "That's not part of the act!" Eve protested.

"I can't help it," Stunts said with a grin. "I'm a crowd-pleaser." He threw his helmet into the air. Then he played to the crowd by holding both his hands up triumphantly. The audience erupted, showering Stunts with cheers and applause.

Eve glanced at Stunts with a confused expression on her face. The kiss had been very intense, and her lips were still tingling.

Then she smiled and waved back at the crowd.

5

*T*he black asphalt of Rexcor Raceway matched the menacing dark buildings lining
the track. The stands were filled with happy spectators, and the infield was packed bumper-to-bumper
with trucks, camper vans, and trailers. Fans stood
on top of their vehicles, waving and cheering.

Vrrooooooommmmmmmmmm!

Several Unlimited Series cars burst out of a turn
and onto a straightaway. Lyle Owens's car was in
the lead, followed by another team's car. Megan
"Spitfire" Fassler zipped after them in third
place. Lyle Owens was sometimes known as The

Collector—he'd joined Team Rexcor after being fired from Team Fastex for dirty driving.

The second-place car surged up beside Lyle, challenging him for the lead. Megan jockeyed for position behind them, looking for an opening to pass both cars.

Suddenly, Lyle veered into the other team's racer beside him. If he'd been hoping that the other team's car would spin out, he was wrong. Instead, it kept pace with him for a stretch, and then slammed into Lyle's car.

Crrrrrruunnnnnch!

Neither driver gave an inch, both still furiously rumbling down the track despite the collisions.

Behind them Megan's car was still entirely blocked.

She reached for the lever that controlled her boosters. "You boys can swap all the paint you want," Megan hollered, "but I'm going through!" She pulled the lever.

Whoooooooooshhhh!

Her turbojet boosters exploded with blasts of flame. Megan soared into the air, sailing over the two cars cruising side by side in front of her.

Megan landed back on the asphalt just in front of the electronic flag board. As she swept beneath the board, the checkered flag flashed on the huge monitor, confirming what she already knew.

She was a winner!

Up in the media room high above Rexcor Raceway, Sports Network Interglobal Television co-anchor Pat Anther was setting up for an interview with Megan. Megan sat quietly on a long couch as Pat grabbed a microphone and hooked a communicator onto her ear, slightly squashing her big blond hairdo. She fussed with a pin on her jacket that read SNIT.

"We're very excited to have gotten the first interview with Megan Fassler—better known to her fans as Spitfire," Pat chirped into the microphone, smiling widely for the camera. "Megan has just won a very tense race, one of the last of the season. That flying finish was so exciting, Megan. We saw some very dedicated driving out of you today."

"Thanks, Pat," Megan replied. "I'm glad to be here."

Now Pat Anther shifted closer to Megan on the couch, her voice getting lower. "It's been a heroic struggle for you, hasn't it, Megan?" Pat asked in a very serious voice. "Coming back from your crash earlier in the season."

"Well," Megan replied, "I couldn't have done it without the support of my father and my crew and my Fastex teammates—"

Suddenly Pat's eyes went blank and she covered her communications earpiece with her hand. She

listened for a moment, then turned back to Megan.

"I'm sorry, uh, Megan," she said. "But we have to go now to my co-anchor, Mike Hauger. He's got an exclusive interview with Carlos 'Stunts' Rey!"

Across the room, Mike Hauger and another camera operator pushed up next to Stunts, who was busy signing autographs for a crowd of admiring fans. Mike leaned over and stuck a microphone in Stunts's face. "Carlos," Mike asked, "how do you handle splitting your career between Unlimited Series racing and stunt driving?"

"*No hay problema*, Mike," Stunts replied with a grin.

Megan watched the interview from the other side of the room. She scowled at Stunts. He was getting all the attention, and he hadn't even won!

No hay problema, Stunts had said.

"Yeah, right," Megan muttered sarcastically.

Stunts wasn't giving his all to Team Fastex.

And that was becoming a *big* problem.

6

*T*he *Team Fastex simulator room* owed its advanced technology to the design genius of Megan Fassler. Drivers strapped into the virtual reality cockpits lining the room actually felt as if they were racing in an Unlimited Series car. It was the next best thing to reality—and some said even better.

Flyer, Megan, and Charger were wearing their VR helmets, waiting for the simulation to start. Next to them, Stunts's empty simulator seemed like a hollow shell.

Duck Dunaka stood on one side of the room, peering at the VR simulator gauges and making notes on a clipboard.

The door to the simulator room opened and Jack Fassler entered. In addition to being the president of Fassler Technologies and the owner of Team Fastex, Jack was also Megan's father. Everybody turned to look at him. When Jack walked into a room, people always stared. He had the aura of a powerful general.

Jack glanced around the room, looking puzzled. "Where's Carlos?" he asked.

Duck didn't look up from his clipboard. He just jerked his thumb over his shoulder, directing Jack to the wall behind them.

Jack turned to look at what Duck had pointed out.

On a wall-mounted TV, Mike Hauger was doing an interview in front of a grandstand.

Grabbing a remote off a metal table, Jack turned up the sound on the TV.

Mike Hauger was in the middle of an announcement. "We're all here today to watch the hottest stunt team in America!" Mike said. "Eve Kildare and Carlos 'Stunts' Rey are ready to thrill the crowd with their high-flying daredevil acrobatics!"

Jack frowned, irritated. He snapped the TV off with the push of a button. "The crowd may be thrilled," he said, "but I'm most definitely not."

The temporary grandstand shook with the stomping of the crowd's feet. The bleachers were overflowing with cheering fans who had come to watch Stunts and Eve perform. Along the edge of the empty field where the daredevils would show their stuff, hundreds of folding chairs had been set up. All were filled with excited spectators. Lines of cars, trucks, and camper vans bordered the field, and fans had climbed on top of their vehicles for a better view.

For this event, Stunts and Eve were both in Unlimited Series cars. Stunts waved once to the crowd before he and Eve gunned their engines.

Vrroooooooommmmmmmmmmm!

The two stunt drivers charged up a long ramp in front of the grandstand, launching off the end side by side at an awesome speed.

Their cars soared through the air, higher than any stunt they'd pulled before.

Then both Stunts and Eve fired their maneuvering jets at the same time. With stunning bravery, the two drivers swung into barrel rolls, flipping toward each other. Stunts rolled high toward Eve, and Eve rolled low toward Stunts. They came so close together in the air that the crowd gasped when their car doors nearly grazed each other. But they managed to trade sides in the sky without colliding.

Eve and Stunts thumped down on the landing ramp. The crowd went nuts with screams and applause.

But the show was not over.

Almost immediately, Stunts fired his side boosters. His car tilted up on two wheels.

On Stunts's cue, Eve blasted her boosters, too. In a second, her car was up on two wheels as well.

Eve and Stunts flung down the old track, weaving back and forth, each on two wheels. They danced around each other in their cars as they zoomed across the asphalt, barely missing each other. They performed their incredible stunt as gracefully as figure skaters.

With a smile, Eve glanced over at Stunts as he wove around her on two wheels. "I have to admit I had my doubts about taking on a partner," Eve told Stunts over the radio. "But you're good—very good."

Stunts returned Eve's smile when his car swerved past hers again. "Even the best of us needs a partner," he said. "When it's the *right* partner."

Eve had to duck her head so that Stunts wouldn't see her blushing.

7

*T*hat night, Garner Rexton ordered Eve to show up at his office on the top floor of the enormous Rexcor Corporation tower. Eve arrived promptly at the time Garner had requested, and she sat down in an uncomfortable chair opposite him.

Garner clasped his hands on top of the vast black desk. "I want a full report," he told Eve.

Eve cleared her throat. "I think Carlos is—" She glanced away, her face reddening. She was blushing again, but this time she had no way to hide it. "I think he may be falling in love with me," Eve told Garner flatly.

Garner raised his dark eyebrows. "And what about you?" he asked.

Eve looked down at her hands, blushing once again.

"Are you falling in love with him?" Garner demanded to know.

Eve took a deep breath, and met Garner's gaze with a look of determination. "We had an agreement," she said. "When I take on a job, nothing stands in the way."

"And when will the job be done?" Garner asked. "When will Carlos Rey leave Team Fastex?"

Eve shook her head. "It may not be easy to get him to quit," she said. "It could cause a lot of trouble with the team."

"That's the whole idea," Garner said. He smiled cruelly. "The more trouble, the better."

The next day, Stunts buzzed down the roads of New Motor City on his motorcycle. He skidded to a stop in front of the tall white building that served as Fastex Corporation headquarters. Stunts pulled off his helmet and leaped from the motorcycle. He hurried toward the entrance, carrying his helmet tucked underneath his arm.

Just as Stunts reached the steps that led to the front door, Jack and Megan Fassler walked out.

Jack stared at Stunts coldly. "If you're trying to make the team meeting, you can slow down," Jack said. "We finished ten minutes ago."

"Sorry, Jack," Stunts apologized with a grin. "I had a show to do."

Megan frowned at Stunts, cutting him dead. "You're wasting your talent with those stunt shows!" she told him. "You're taking unnecessary risks just for money and fame—"

"Hey," Stunts argued. "Money and fame is the name of the game!" He pointed at himself with his thumb. "I'm going to be somebody—rich and famous! If you can't handle that, then you can just pull off the road and park it."

"What you're doing is hurting the team, Carlos," Jack said. "And I can't have that. You have to make a choice. You're either a stunt driver or a member of Team Fastex. You can't be both."

Megan and Jack pushed past Stunts and headed down the headquarters steps.

Stunts turned to look at them as they walked away. Worry flickered across his face. "Maybe a stunt could help the team!" he called after them.

Megan and Jack stopped. Slowly they turned around to face Stunts.

Stunts took a step toward them. "What if before the next race, the whole team did a really big jump?" he asked. "The publicity would be huge!"

Megan glared at Stunts as though he had lost his mind. "We're racers," she said flatly. "Not stunt drivers—"

"Wait a minute, Megan," Jack said, interrupting his daughter. "You've seen how the public reacts to those jumps." He studied Stunts carefully. "What did you have in mind?" he asked.

Megan groaned, rolling her eyes in disbelief. "Dad?"

Jack and Stunts started walking toward the building. "We put up ramps right in front of the starting line," Stunts explained, thinking fast. "And all four cars go straight up in the air, as high as we can. . . ."

8

*T*hat night, Eve and Stunts met up at Stunts's apartment to talk about plans for the big Team Fastex stunt show.

Eve sat on the living room sofa with the remains of a fast food meal on the coffee table in front of her, listening to Stunts's ideas. Stunts paced around the room, too excited to sit still. The walls in the apartment were covered with posters and blown-up pictures of Stunts and his car.

"Then we fire our jets to flip our cars' noses down, back toward the ramps," Stunts was saying. He gestured dramatically to illustrate the stunt he was describing. "We can use drogue chutes to slow our fall and just follow the ramps down to the ground again."

"I don't know about *all* of Team Fastex doing a jump," Eve said carefully. She shifted on the sofa. "I thought we were a team—just you and me."

Stunts sat down beside her. "We *are* a team, Eve," he told her. "But I owe Team Fastex—they gave me a chance to drive for the Unlimited Series."

He looked away, hesitating for a moment as he tried to figure out a way to explain to Eve how he felt about his team. It wasn't just that he felt like he owed them something. . . .

Stunts flashed Eve his famous grin. "Besides," he said, "they're my friends!"

Garner Rexton's office seemed ten times creepier at night than it did in the daytime. Only one light was on in the giant room—a bright spotlight hanging from the ceiling. Eve stood in a pool of harsh light in front of Garner's desk. Garner himself, sitting in his desk chair, was hidden in shadows.

"Stunts won't leave Team Fastex," Eve explained to her boss. "He's too loyal."

Garner leaned forward so that his face caught the light. "We had an agreement," he told her. "If Carlos Rey leaves Fastex, your debt to me is forgiven. And if he doesn't—"

A worried expression crossed Eve's pretty face.

Garner smiled, enjoying her discomfort. "Do I need to remind you that you owe me more money than you can ever possibly repay?" he asked.

"He would've quit, Mr. Rexton," Eve said quickly. "If Jack Fassler hadn't agreed to this team jump—"

"Wait," Garner said, interrupting her. He rubbed his chin, lost in thought. "All four Team Fastex drivers in a dangerous stunt jump . . ."

Eve watched anxiously as Garner swiveled his chair to the side and stared into the darkness. For a moment he seemed to vanish into the silent shadows.

"Fastex could lose four drivers instead of one . . ." Garner said slowly, thinking aloud. "If something tragic should happen, that is."

He leaned back into the light, and Eve gulped when she saw the deep hatred in his glittering eyes.

Garner folded his hands on his desk. "And Eve?" he asked in a dangerous, thick voice. "We're going to make certain that something tragic *does* happen, aren't we?"

Stunned, Eve couldn't think of anything to say in reply. She stuck her hands into her pockets so that Garner wouldn't see them shaking in fear.

"Imagine the headlines," Garner said, opening his arms wide. "Team Fastex Drivers Lost in Publicity Stunt."

"That wasn't part of our agreement," Eve protested softly.

Garner stood up behind his desk and walked toward a huge dark window. "You won't have to sabotage the jump yourself," he said, peering out into the darkness. "Just tell Jack Fassler you want a fireworks display during the stunt."

Garner peered through his office window, looking out at the starry sky. "I have a fireworks expert you can use," he said.

Eve stared at Garner nervously. "An expert, sir?" she asked. "Is he any good?"

"Oh, yes," Garner replied. "He's the best." With a small mean laugh, Garner turned his back to her and sank back down in his chair.

Eve's blood ran cold when Garner swung around again to face her.

"And he also does demolition work," Garner added.

9

Mike Hauger and Pat Anther smiled into the camera. Far in the background, the lights of Big River Raceway glowed warmly. Right behind Mike and Pat was the center of the racetrack infield, where four steep ramps loomed up behind the announcers. Lined up together in a row, the ends of the steel ramps stuck straight up into the air, gleaming in the bright spotlights focused on them. The ramps curved gently where they met the grass of the infield.

Mike Hauger let out a low whistle. "Tonight's race

may be overshadowed by the big prerace four-car stunt jump," he told SNIT's audience.

"That's right, Mike," Pat Anther agreed cheerfully. "Team owner Jack Fassler has promised a spectacle that no one will ever forget!"

Near the ramps, Eve nervously watched the sinister-looking fireworks man as he kneeled down to put the finishing touches on his launchers. "Is everything all set?" she asked.

"Just like Mr. Rexton ordered," the explosives expert confirmed. "The fireworks were supposed to go off over the infield lake, but I've made a few . . . *adjustments.*"

Eve turned away, biting her lip nervously. She figured that the less she knew about the expert's "adjustments," the better off she'd be.

At the beginning of the long straightaway that led directly to the ramps, the Team Fastex drivers climbed into their cars.

"I've double-checked everything," Megan called to her teammates. "I've even run through the jump on the simulator—"

"Stop worrying, Megan," Stunts said. "Eve's the best."

Megan put her hands on her hips. "We're trusting her with our lives, Carlos," she replied.

"She can have mine anytime she wants," he said with a grin.

• • •

Team Rexcor—Lyle, Specter, Zorina, and Junker—watched jealously as they stood by their cars in pit row.

"Big jump, big deal," Zorina grumbled, tossing her head. "I could do a stunt that'd make you forget there ever was an Eve Kildare!"

"Maybe we should talk to the boss about doing a Rexcor stunt show," Lyle suggested.

Junker nodded. *"Ja!"* he exclaimed in his deep voice. "I will be telling him myself how we should be jumping like these stunts! Garner Rexton will obey Junker!"

Specter glanced warily at Junker. "Maybe somebody *else* should talk to the boss," he said.

Megan drove her car onto the track for a few warm-up laps. She activated her radio as she steered. "I still don't like this, Stunts," Megan said. "This isn't what Unlimited Series racing is all about."

"Hey, Spitfire—lighten up," Stunts replied over the radio. He took one hand off the wheel and waved it in annoyance. "It's a show—a spectacle! That's what the crowd comes to see."

"Megan's right," Charger added from inside his car. "This isn't racing."

Flyer didn't join his teammates' discussion. He was sweating, feeling the strange sensation of his mysterious problem—the same problem that had forced him to drop out of the Air Force. Flyer steered with one hand as he examined the other. It was shaking.

"But I'm ready to try anything other drivers do!" Charger continued.

Flyer put his shaking hand back on the steering wheel. He gripped the wheel tightly to stop his hand from trembling. There was no way he was going to let his problem stop him from performing tonight. No way.

Eve spoke into a handheld portable radio. "Carlos, everything's ready for the jump," she said, trying to hide the worry in her voice. "Good luck."

"You sound as nervous as Megan," Stunts replied. "Relax. It'll be a piece of cake."

The four Fastex cars cruised around the track, gaining speed as they approached the ramps again.

"Okay, Fastex!" Stunts hollered over the radio. "Let's get this show on the road!

Vrroooooooommmmmmmmmm!

All the Team Fastex drivers slammed down their accelerator pedals, blazing toward the ramps.

The only light in Garner Rexton's dark office came from the big-screen TV hanging in the corner. He

smiled coldly as the Team Fastex cars on the TV screen sizzled toward the ramps. Although Garner had no love for stunt driving, he wouldn't have missed this particular pregame show for a billion dollars.

"This will be the stunt to end all stunts," Garner whispered to himself. "And the end of Team Fastex!"

10

*T*he four Team Fastex cars suddenly peeled off the track, each hurtling toward a different ramp set up in the infield.

The fireworks man bent over his controls, ready to start the show. Eve rushed over to him. "I changed my mind!" she shouted. "Don't set off the fireworks!"

But as Eve reached for the controls, the fireworks expert grabbed her in his greasy hands.

"It's too late to stop it!" the expert growled. "We've got to get away!" He let go of Eve and ran toward the nearest exit.

Truly frightened now, Eve watched as the Team Fastex cars surged up the ramps and shot straight into the night sky.

"Carlos!" she cried helplessly as the fireworks launched. "No!"

The four Fastex cars reached the topmost point of their jump, high in the air. The fireworks rockets sizzled up to meet them.

The crowd in the stands roared happily, oohing and ahhing at the red, white, and blue fireworks reflecting on the infield lake.

But then the fireworks began exploding inches away from the Team Fastex cars in the air! The crowd's roar turned to screams of fear.

Charger felt a big jolt as explosions rocked his car. "Hey!" he hollered. "That's a little too close!"

Megan's car was knocked sideways as fireworks blew up around her. She cried out, startled.

Flyer quickly pulled a lever to open his car's wings. He spiraled downward as fireworks burst right outside his window. "Use your drogue chutes!" Flyer ordered his teammates. "Head for the ramps as planned!"

Stunts pulled the lever that released his drogue chute. But the moment the chute expanded behind him, a blazing rocket zoomed through it, shredding the thin material. Stunts's car plummeted.

Trying not to panic, Megan also released her car's chute. As the chute snaked out behind her, fire-

works whizzed past it, causing it to tangle. The drogue chute trailed uselessly after her car like a tail. Megan began to tumble toward the ground far below.

Thinking quickly, Stunts threw another lever on his control panel.

Whooosh!

Stunts's maneuvering jets blasted out funnels of flame. His car swiveled in the air, heading back on course toward a ramp.

As Megan fell through the exploding sky in her car, she struggled to reach a lever on her dash. "Got to regain control," she muttered. She pulled the lever and her jets erupted with blasts of fire. But instead of turning her in the air, Megan used her side-mounted rockets like brakes, slowing her fall toward the ground.

Meanwhile, Charger had released his drogue chute. A large rocket went off right beside the chute as it unfolded—and set it on fire! Alarms ringing in his car, Charger dropped from the sky like a comet, fiery tail and all.

Flyer's heart leaped in his chest when he saw Charger's car falling and dragging the flaming chute. "Get outta there, Charger!" he yelled. "Eject!"

Charger fought to regain control of his tumbling car. "I'm not giving up on my car!" he replied through gritted teeth.

11

H*is wings fully extended, Flyer* sailed down toward Charger's car. As Flyer got closer, he launched his grappling hook.

Claaaaangggg!

He speared Charger's car with the hook. Flyer fired his turbojet boosters and towed Charger's car, with its flaming drogue chute, over the infield lake. Charger skipped like a stone across the lake until his car pulled free from the grappling hook. Then the flames hissed out on the chute as Charger splashed into the water.

Megan had succeeded at slowing down in the air

by using her side-mounted rockets as brakes. Adjusting her booster jets, she tried to steer her car toward one of the waiting ramps.

But then Megan was hit by another fireworks blast! She started spinning out of control, tumbling through the sky.

Megan let out a short shriek. She punched a button on her control panel. Her Rescue Racer ejected out of the car with her inside.

The Rescue Racer glided over the pits, bouncing along the roofs of haulers.

Meanwhile, Megan's abandoned car crashed down in the track's refueling area. It exploded, igniting the fuel stored nearby. A huge fireball rose up in the night sky.

The crowd in the grandstands screamed in panic. The horrified fans barely noticed that Stunts had cruised down one of the ramps and onto the track. He was the only member of Team Fastex to have made a successful return as the jump plan intended. But for this trick, Stunts didn't receive any cheers. Instead, the audience ran for the exits in a terrified mob.

Eve rushed over to another team's Unlimited Series racer in the pits. The name painted on the car was BOMBER. She scrambled in.

One of Team Bomber's crew members nearly dropped the handheld radio he was carrying when he saw Eve climb in the car. "Hey!" he shouted.

Stunts saw the car roaring out of the pits, heading for an exit tunnel.

"Somebody's stealing our car!" the Team Bomber crew member hollered over all radio channels.

"I see him!" Stunts squawked back over the radio. "It must be that fireworks guy! Tell Eve Kildare I'm going after him!"

The stolen car plunged out of the stadium through the exit tunnel.

Stunts sped after it, swearing, "He won't get away from me!"

The explosion from Megan's car didn't just blow up one fuel tank—it set off a chain reaction of explosions throughout the infield. One blast crumpled the bases of two camera towers near the refueling area.

Krrrrrrreeeeeeeeeeeeeeeeeeeeeeee!

With huge metallic groans, the towers slowly toppled, sending off showers of blue sparks and broken glass.

A NASCAR official wearing a headset and carrying a clipboard was standing a few feet away from the towers. He dropped his clipboard and stared up in terror as one of the shorn steel towers lurched straight toward him.

12

*T*he NASCAR official covered his face with his hands, waiting for the fatal crunch. Megan's Rescue Racer zipped over to the frightened official and skidded to a stop beside him. "Get in!" Megan screamed.

When the NASCAR official didn't move, Megan reached out of her racer and grabbed the official's shirtfront. With a sharp yank, Megan pulled him inside.

They tore away just as the camera tower smashed right where the NASCAR official had been standing.

Overhead, Flyer zoomed by, still trailing his grappling hook. He dived down and snagged the other falling camera tower. He tugged it aside, stopping the tower from falling on a parked fuel truck.

Duck drove the Team Fastex IMP over to the crumpled tower. He quickly hooked up the IMP to the intact fuel truck, backing it away from the fire.

Above the track, a red fire-fighting helicopter circled. Its propellers whirred as it dropped fire retardant on the flames.

A few blocks outside Big River Raceway, the brand-new streets of New Motor City were mostly deserted, since most of the people had been at the race. The crowds fleeing the raceway hadn't yet made it this far.

Vrroooooooommmmmmmmmmm!

Eve—in the Team Bomber Unlimited Series car—dashed into an empty intersection, skidding through a ninety-degree turn onto another street. She blazed down the road at top speed.

A second later, Stunts slid through the same turn and charged after the stolen car.

Eve's car careened onto a street by the rushing river. She glanced back in alarm toward Stunts—he was gaining on her. "Why did it have to be him?"

Eve asked herself softly. She jerked the steering wheel, turning the car hard toward the river.

With a roar, Eve launched off the bank, leaping out over the water. The Bomber Team car landed on a row of barges being hauled downstream. The barges were heaped with scrap metal and junked cars piled alongside wide pathways.

Eve breathed a sigh of relief. "I got away," she congratulated herself. "He's good, but he's not *that* good."

On the edge of the river, Stunts rumbled up the bank. His car breezed into the air . . . and slammed down on the barge behind Eve.

"No!" Eve cried.

Eve plunged down a long pathway on the giant barge, with Stunts hot on her bumper. A sloping pile of crushed cars appeared ahead of her as the pathway narrowed. She used the ragged slope to go up on two side wheels, grazing past a big heap of scrap metal.

Stunts fired his jets. His car tilted up on two wheels, too, so he could follow her down the path.

Up ahead of Eve was the end of the barge. She blasted her booster rockets, and jumped to another long barge that was passing in the opposite direction, heading upriver. This barge wasn't as cluttered as the first—only a pile of coal sat on the far end.

Firing his turbojet boosters, Stunts easily made the leap to the next barge. He was still gaining on the car ahead of him.

The two Unlimited Series cars hurtled down the barge, gaining speed.

Eve was getting close to the heap of coal. She took a deep breath, and used the heap of coal like a ramp to soar over the river.

She was heading right toward a bridge! Eve sailed through the air, hoping she would make it safely to the bridge's roadway.

Kaa-raaaaaaash!

Eve smashed into the side of the bridge just inches below the roadway. Her car plummeted into the water with a tremendous splash.

Stunts blasted his turbojet booster as he spurted off the coal ramp on the barge and sailed toward the bridge. Then he launched his grappling hook.

The hook snared the crumpled bumper of Eve's partially sunken car.

Traffic screeched to a stop as Stunts landed on the bridge. Digging into the pavement of the bridge with traction spikes, Stunts revved his engine.

Vrrooooooooommmmmmmmmm!

Slowly Stunts backed up on the bridge. The grappling hook line went taut. Inch by inch, Eve's battered car was hauled out of the water, toward the bridge.

As soon as Eve had made it safely to the bridge's roadway, Stunts leaped out of his car and ran to her.

Expecting to see the fireworks expert, Stunts threw open the car door with BOMBER written on the side.

13

*T*he shock Stunts felt when he saw Eve behind the wheel nearly made him drop to the asphalt. His stomach twisted in disappointment. Eve sat in the car, her face turned away from Stunts. From what he could see, she seemed soaked and dazed, but not seriously hurt.

"Eve?" he asked, helping her out of the bashed-up car. "Why were you running away?"

Avoiding Stunts's eyes, Eve shrugged. Her lips were pressed together so tightly that they were turning white.

An expression of realization flickered over

Stunts's face. "You knew, didn't you?" he asked slowly, sounding amazed—and hurt. "About the sabotaged jump, the fireworks . . . You knew all along what was going to happen."

Eve looked down at her feet. Her guilt was obvious from the sad way she hung her head.

"I owed someone," Eve said flatly. "I can't tell you his name." She glanced up at Stunts. "If I didn't do what he wanted, he would've ruined my whole career!" Eve swallowed, trying to control her misery. "No money, no fame . . . I can't live without those, Carlos."

Stunts closed his eyes for a moment, fully understanding the pressure she'd faced. He had felt very similar temptations himself.

"I have to *be* somebody," Eve said.

A flush turned Stunts's cheeks red. Eve's story had hit too close to home, and he felt ashamed of himself. "I said the same thing—" he began. "But I was *wrong*, Eve. You don't need money to be somebody. And you don't have to be famous because—"

Eeee-oh! Eeee-oh! Eeee-oh! Eeee-oh!

When Eve heard the siren, she glanced at the approaching police car in fear.

"It takes only one person to make you feel important," Stunts finished quietly.

The police car rushed over to them, its siren blaring. It screeched to a stop on the bridge.

Eve looked over at Stunts, her eyes wide. "Are you going to turn me in?" she asked softly.

"If I have to," Stunts answered. He closed his eyes for a second and shook his head. "If I have to," he repeated sadly.

Eve sighed. "I'll tell them what I did," she promised. She gave Stunts a final look and then walked away toward the police car, where two policemen were getting out.

Stunts watched her for a moment, and then he turned away, his expression heartbroken. "Adios, partner," Stunts whispered.

Whup-whup-whup-whup-whup-whup!

Suddenly, a helicopter arrived, its propellers whirring. It landed on the bridge near Stunts.

Flyer, Megan, and Charger leaped out of the chopper, and hurried over to Stunts. They gathered around him, looking puzzled.

Charger glanced over at the police car. "What's going on, Stunts?" he asked.

Stunts checked out the situation at the police car. Eve gave him a last longing look as one of the policemen put handcuffs on her. Then she turned toward the police car and got in.

Megan shook her head. "It wasn't an accident, was it?" she asked. "The fireworks going wrong, I mean."

Stunts didn't reply—he was too busy watching Eve.

Megan studied Stunts's face, wincing a little at his sad, lonely expression. "Why did she do it, Carlos?" she asked.

Abruptly, Stunts turned to meet Megan's gaze. "Some people get carried away with fame and success," he said. He glanced again toward the police car, which was leaving with Eve inside, and then he looked sadly down at his feet. "It's not easy," he said softly, "learning how to handle it."

All the Team Fastex drivers were silent for a moment, solemnly thinking about Stunts's words.

Then Stunts heaved a big sigh. "Come on," he said. "We've got a race to run."

Flyer, Megan, and Charger watched sympathetically as Stunts walked to his car and got in.

Vrroooooooommmmmmmmmm!

The engine roared to life, and Stunts drove away.

He headed for Big River Raceway, with the Motorsphere rising above it. Over the jagged New Motor City skyline, Stunts could see wispy clouds of smoke still floating up from the burnt infield.

The smoke rose slowly into the sky and faded away.

14

A *few weeks later,* Rexcor Race-
way was hosting the fourth-to-last race of the season. The crowd was at maximum capacity, the
stands were overflowing with screaming fans. The
race was almost over, and the lead cars were heading into the final turn.

Vrrrrrrrrrooooooooommmmmmm!

Lyle Owens, Junker, and Flyer rounded the turn,
drafting in a line one behind the other.

Suddenly Flyer pulled out of line, trying to pass.

Junker glanced in his rearview mirror. *"Nein,
Flieger!"* the burly foreign driver blurted out. "It is

Rexcor's day to be winning!" He swerved slightly, scratching up against Flyer's car.

For a few moments, the two cars ground together, swapping paint. But then they pulled apart, zooming along the track side by side.

Junker grinned with maniacal happiness. "This time it is you I am junking!" he yelled. He veered closer, leering out his window at Flyer.

Flyer pulled a lever, expanding his car's wings. "You missed your flight again, Junker!" Flyer hollered in reply.

As Junker closed in, about to collide with Flyer, Flyer's car went airborne. Junker's car slipped underneath, missing him completely.

Crrrrrruunnnnnch!

Junker scraped along the wall. He wrestled with his steering, crying out in alarm as his car spun out.

Lyle neared the finish line, smiling in satisfaction. "Looks like I'm about to collect a first-place finish," he congratulated himself. The road ahead to the electronic flag board seemed clear.

Until Flyer's car sailed in from above.

"Hey!" Lyle yelled.

With a screech of tires, Flyer's car landed in front of Owens. Its wings retracted as it roared across the finish line.

The checkered flag flashed on the electronic board.

Flyer had won!

• • •

In the Team Fastex hauler, on the way home after the race, the drivers watched the SNIT race recap on TV.

Mike Hauger smiled into the camera. "It was a big win this afternoon for Team Fastex driver Steve 'Flyer' Sharp," he announced.

Mike Hauger turned to Pat Anther, who was sitting beside him at the SNIT anchor desk. "Mike," Pat said, "Today's win puts the enigmatic former pilot in reach of the Unlimited Series driver championship."

Gathered around the TV, Flyer, Charger, Stunts, and Megan let out a loud cheer.

"Enigmatic," Flyer repeated. "What's that supposed to mean?"

"Mysterious," Megan replied.

"No," Stunts told Flyer with a grin. "It means you give a lousy interview, *compadre*. You've got to learn how to act like a champion."

Flyer stood up. "If you could drive with your *mouth*, Carlos," he shot back, "you'd win every race!"

Stunts looked annoyed as Flyer stomped out of the drivers' lounge.

Charger raised his eyebrows at Stunts. "You can teach him to *talk* like a champion," he said, "and I'll show you both how to *drive* like one."

Stunts smirked. "The only thing you're gonna be

doing is watching me give those championship interviews," he told Charger.

"If I see you anywhere," Charger replied, "it'll be in my rearview mirror."

While they were busy dissing each other, the Team Fastex hauler drove past a guardhouse along-side a gate in a barbed-wire fence.

A sign over the gate read, PINE RIDGE TESTING GROUNDS.

The Team Fastex hauler drove off down the road. Only a few seconds after it had passed, alarms blared inside the compound.

15

Nobody in the Team Fastex hauler heard the alarms—or saw what happened next.

The gate clanged shut and two soldiers rushed into position, barring the way in or out of the compound.

Suddenly, a monster truck rumbled up the highway to the gate. A passenger leaned out the window of the monster truck. His name was Forrest, and he was dressed in black military gear. Forrest tossed a gas grenade out the window. It plopped down between the two soldiers guarding the gate, releasing a cloud of knockout gas.

Forrest quickly pulled his head back into the monster truck. The huge vehicle roared off, its tires squealing.

One of the soldiers managed to stagger out of the gas cloud. He grabbed a phone hanging on the wall of the guardhouse. "We're under attack—" the soldier reported groggily. "Some kind of sleep gas . . . "

Then the soldier dropped the phone and slumped to the ground.

Vvvrrroooooooooooommmmmmmmm!

Inside the compound, the sound of giant engines revving shook the night. The slumped soldier was suddenly flooded with dazzling light. Blinding headlights glared out of the blackness inside the compound.

Smmaaaaaaash!

A second monster truck crashed through the gate, demolishing it before rumbling down the highway, following Forrest's massive vehicle.

The Team Fastex hauler pulled into the parking lot of the Greasy G truck stop. The low building had a giant sign hanging above it, which showed a huge, fat hamburger with a garish flashing *G* on it. Blinking neon grease dripped from the burger. The parking lot around the truck stop sprawled for hun-

Daredevil Eve Kildare is back with a new partner--Carlos "Stunts" Rey--attempting another death-defying feat.

Eve's giving her signal...they're ready to go!

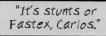

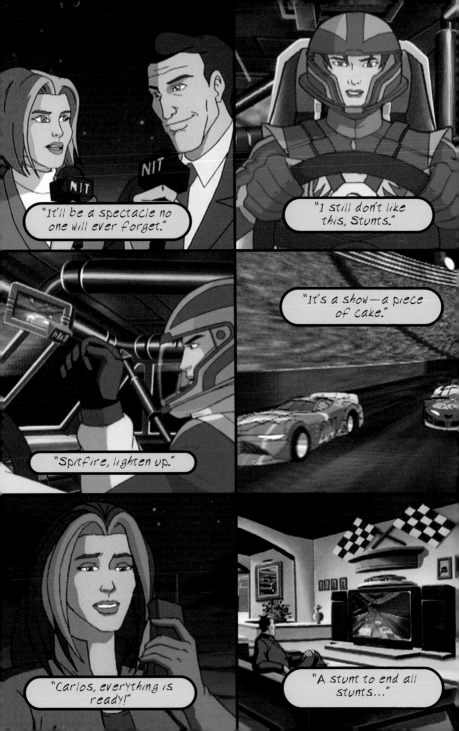

dreds of feet around, with lots of semi trucks idling on the asphalt. A strip of gasoline tanks and pumps lined the far edge of the lot.

Right after the Team Fastex hauler came to a stop in the Greasy G lot, two police cars streaked by in the opposite direction, sirens wailing.

Megan opened the hauler's door and stepped out, sniffing the air with disgust. Flyer, Stunts, and Charger appeared in the doorway behind her.

"Not another truck stop!" Megan complained.

Duck Dunaka and the driver jumped out of the hauler's cab. "This place has the best greasy food in America!" Duck exclaimed, smacking his lips. He hurried toward the truck stop's entrance.

The hauler driver turned and called out to Duck. "Hey! Are we gonna get gas here?" he asked.

"Probably," Megan muttered sarcastically. "If we eat this food."

As Team Fastex pushed their way inside the greasy truck stop restaurant, the second monster truck was still roaring down the highway. The two police cars were now hot on its massive bumper. The first monster truck with Forrest inside had made it to safety.

Inside the second monster truck were two more men dressed in paramilitary gear. Wilson was driving, and Russell was sitting in the passenger seat. They both looked like rough, dangerous men.

Russell picked up a handheld radio. "We've got the guidance component," he said. A small electronic gadget bristling with wires and circuits rested on the seat next to Russell. "But the cops are right on our tail!"

The first monster truck had parked in the shadows at the side of a lonely country road, totally hidden from view.

A very scary looking man named Stiles sat in the driver's seat of the hidden monster truck. He was dressed the same as the others, but he was older, and obviously in charge. "Stash the guidance component somewhere safe," Stiles gruffly told Russell over the radio. "I'll come back for it later."

Russell and Wilson roared down the highway, pulling ahead of the cops. Suddenly, the passenger door opened. The monster truck blasted off the highway, bouncing onto a rough dirt road. Russell jumped out, carrying the component.

The two police cars skidded on the highway and followed the second monster truck onto the dirt road.

Russell crouched in the shadows under a tree, watching as the police cars drove off into the distance chasing Wilson, their sirens fading.

Whup-whup-whup-whup-whup-whup!

Russell glanced up. A military helicopter passed overhead, tracking the police cars, its searchlight glaring along the dirt road.

16

*I*nside the Greasy G truck stop, Duck took a huge bite from a dripping cheeseburger. "You guys sure you don't want a fried pie with your burger?" he asked with his mouth full.

Megan, Stunts, Charger, and Flyer all shook their heads as Duck shoved the rest of the burger into his mouth.

Megan looked grossed out as she stared at the half-eaten plate of food in front of her. "I think I'll go back to the hauler," she said, "while I can still walk." She stood up.

As Megan walked away from the table, Duck eyed

her food. "Don't you want your onion rings?" he called after her. When she didn't reply, he grabbed a handful from Megan's plate.

The Greasy G parking lot was surrounded by forest on three sides. Russell emerged from the trees and cautiously made his way between the parked trucks, vans, and cars.

The driver of the Team Fastex hauler had stayed with the big vehicle to refuel it. Finished with that task, he closed the door to the hauler's cab and walked toward the restaurant to catch up with the others.

Nearby, Russell watched from the shadows. He slipped the component into a small magnetic box. Sneaking up to the Team Fastex hauler, he sneaked inside and closed the door behind him.

Megan walked around the hauler, coming from the diner.

Inside the hauler's main compartment, Russell opened an access panel in the ceiling. Through the open hatch, he could see the underside of one of the Unlimited Series cars stored overhead. "Team Fastex can get this thing past the cops for us," Russell muttered to himself.

He reached up through the open hatch to place the component under the car. With a quiet *thunk*,

the magnetic box attached to the bottom of the car. On the side of the car was the name FLYER. Russell closed the panel.

Megan walked up to the hauler door and reached for the handle.

Russell had just shut the access panel when he heard the door open.

He whirled around.

And drew his gun.

Megan took one step into the hauler.

Eeee-oh! Eeee-oh! Eeee-oh! Eeee-oh!

She paused when she heard the police sirens. With a glance over her shoulder, Megan checked out the commotion on the highway.

Russell hid just behind the door, with his gun aimed at the doorway, ready to fire.

Megan walked away from the half-open hauler door, and headed over to a man she'd spotted by the gas pumps.

The man was obviously a tourist—wearing shorts, a garish Hawaiian shirt, and sandals with socks. He was holding a gas nozzle, getting ready to fill up his minivan.

"Do you know what's going on?" Megan asked him.

The tourist smiled at her. "I heard there was a break-in at some big government lab," he replied.

Behind them, Russell slinked out of the hauler. He strode away quickly.

Megan hiked back over to the hauler, leaving the tourist pumping gas.

On the other side of the minivan where the tourist couldn't see, Russell quietly opened the minivan door. He crept inside.

Megan went inside the hauler, closing the door behind her.

The tourist removed the gas pump nozzle from the tank and turned to put it back on the pump.

Vrrrrrrrrooooommmm!

Suddenly the minivan engine started. The tourist whipped around in surprise. "Hey!" he shouted.

With a screech of tires, the minivan took off. Russell steered it out of the parking lot and onto the highway.

As he drove, Russell pulled out his portable radio. "I hid the guidance component," he reported to Stiles. "It's in a Team Fastex race car—blue and yellow."

"What's the name on the car?" Stiles asked.

Instead of answering, Russell suddenly let out a startled cry. As the minivan rounded a turn, he was faced with a military roadblock. HumVees and police cars waited in the road with flashing blue lights.

Russell jammed on the brakes.

The van skidded off the road and flipped over in a ditch.

Russell quickly climbed out, leaving his radio behind. He started to stagger away, but stumbled and fell to his knees.

"I need to know the name on the car!" Stiles demanded from the radio inside the minivan.

As Russell struggled to climb to his feet, he was caught in a spotlight from above. The police helicopter had him fixed in its lights.

A military police car screeched to a stop in front of him.

Russell put his hands up.

"I surrender!" he shouted.

17

A *day later, Jack Fassler gathered* all the members of Team Fastex at the Fassler Corporation headquarters. The meeting took place in the spacious conference room on the top floor.

"Our next race is cross-country," Jack announced to the group. "It will take place on the new interstate they're building from New Motor City to the coast."

Jack stood at the head of a long wooden conference table. "It's called the All-American highway," he continued, "and the race is part of its grand opening. NASCAR has decided that one of our people will have the honor of driving the flagship car in the race."

Megan, Stunts, Charger, and Flyer listened attentively, each one eager to be chosen to drive the flagship car.

"To be fair," Jack said, "I decided that whoever finished best in the last race would get to drive the All-American car." Jack stepped over to Flyer and put his hand on his shoulder. "Congratulations, Flyer."

Jealousy flickered over Stunts's and Charger's faces.

"I would've won the last race," Charger protested, "if I hadn't blown my engine!"

"What about me?" Stunts asked. "I look good in red, white, and blue!" He smoothed back his hair, pleased with himself. "But, hey," he said, "I look good in anything."

"I've made my decision, and it's final," Jack said. "Duck's already started repainting Flyer's car."

Inside the busy Team Fastex garage, Duck sat hunched over on a stack of tires, clutching his stomach. He took deep gulps of antacid from a pink bottle and groaned loudly.

Miles McCutchen, Charger's younger brother, was helping out in the garage. "Did you watch the news last night, Duck?" Miles asked. He paused for

a moment from his task—using a sprayer to cover Flyer's blue-and-yellow car with white paint. "Some spies broke into a government lab," Miles said. He sounded thrilled. "They stole a missile guidance system! You drove right past the lab on the way back from the race."

Duck groaned again from where he was sitting on the tires, only half listening.

"Did you see any spies?" Miles asked.

"Did you say something about *fries*?" Duck replied with another groan. His stomach rumbled. Clutching his gut, Duck staggered to his feet. "I've got to make a pit stop," he moaned. "Must be something I ate. . . ." He rushed out of the garage.

Miles shrugged and continued repainting Flyer's car.

18

*S*tiles *peered up at the tall Team* Fastex headquarters building, which was silhouetted against the starry night sky. Stiles, Forrest, Wilson, and a few other men dressed in dark paramilitary garb were gathered around a monster truck parked in the shadows near the headquarters. A week had passed since Russell attached the stolen component to the bottom of Flyer's car.

"The guidance component is hidden in a Team Fastex race car," Stiles told his men. "We don't know who it belongs to, but we do know that it's painted yellow and blue. Find that car!"

Inside the building, Jack and Duck were walking down a corridor toward Jack's office. Duck was holding his stomach.

"Go ahead and start the team meeting without me," Duck said. "I've got to get some more stomach medicine out of my locker."

"How can you have indigestion for a whole week, Duck?" Jack asked.

"Good food stays with you," Duck replied. He hurried down the hall.

In the garage, the Team Fastex race cars were parked in a row. Miles had finished the paint job on Flyer's car—it was now red, white, and blue.

The door to the garage opened quietly, and Stiles slipped inside. He clicked on a masked flashlight and trailed the weak beam over the row of cars.

"Blue and yellow," Stiles whispered, "blue and yellow . . ." He let out a groan of frustration. "There isn't any blue-and-yellow car here!"

Stiles clicked off the light and crossed to the first car, which had SPITFIRE written on it. He got down on his hands and knees to look underneath it. "I'll have to check all of them," Stiles muttered.

Suddenly, Stiles heard the sound of footsteps approaching, and he froze.

Duck walked in and clicked on the lights.

Stiles hunched down, hidden behind Megan's car.

Duck hurried to his locker and retrieved a bottle of antacid. He struggled with it a moment. "Child-proof caps!" Duck complained. He stepped up to a workbench and picked up a torque wrench.

Stiles crept up on Duck.

"I had to get Miles to open the last one," Duck muttered to himself. He put the wrench on the bottle and twisted. The bottle flew out of his hand.

The bottle of antacid medicine clattered across the floor, scattering tablets everywhere. The bottle landed between Stiles's booted feet.

Stiles quickly read the label. "Gas?" he said. "Good idea." He pulled out a knockout gas grenade and flipped it toward Duck.

Foooosh!

Duck was enveloped in a cloud of knockout gas. He coughed, choking. Duck staggered to the wall and pulled a fire alarm, which began wailing as he slumped down to the floor of the garage.

The fire alarm blared as Stiles rushed out of the garage, empty-handed. He climbed into a waiting monster truck, which roared away before the door was shut.

Wilson was driving. Stiles clutched the dash as Wilson threw the truck around a curve, tires squealing.

"We'll have to get the component after the race," Stiles said through gritted teeth.

"NASCAR does a post-race tear-down of the winning cars," Wilson pointed out. "They even inspect some that just finish. What if they find the component?"

Stiles thought for a moment, and then a look of fierce determination crossed his face. "Then we'll have to make sure that no Team Fastex car finishes the race," he said. "It's that simple."

Summoned by the fire alarm, it took only a few minutes for the entire team to rush to the garage. Jack and Megan quickly helped Duck to his feet, while Flyer, Stunts, and Charger checked around the garage.

"Are you all right, Duck?" Jack asked.

Duck sat up. And let out a huge burp in reply.

Megan and Jack turned away in disgust, groaning.

Duck smiled. "Whew!" he said. "Nothing like a little nap to fix you right up!" He scrambled to his feet.

The others stared at him in disbelief.

"Anybody hungry?" Duck asked.

19

*B*ig River Raceway's parking lot was jam-packed with cars, and the entrance to the lot was filled with bumper-to-bumper traffic. Fans from all over the world filed into the grandstands, everybody chattering excitedly about the All-American race.

Hondo "Specter" Hines strode past a line of Unlimited Division cars. All the cars had their hoods up, and mechanics worked on them frantically with whining torque wrenches and banging hammers. Specter pulled out a cell phone as he stepped behind a hauler.

"I want to put twenty thousand dollars on Team Rexcor," Specter said into the phone. He listened for a moment, his face twisting with anger. "To win, of course!" he yelled.

Specter folded up the cell phone and walked quickly away. He rounded the corner of the hauler and ran right into Stiles.

Stiles held up a pen and a race program. "Specter Hines!" Stiles cried with fake enthusiasm. "Can I get your autograph?"

"Sure," Specter replied. "For five dollars, at the Team Rexcor souvenir booth."

Specter tried to push past Stiles, but Stiles raised his pen and—

Whooosh!

Stiles sprayed knockout gas from his pen. Specter went limp.

"Security—" Specter moaned weakly, before slumping into Stiles's arms.

A couple of minutes later, Stiles came out from around the corner of the hauler, zipping himself into Specter's driving suit. He put on Specter's helmet and hurried toward the Team Rexcor pits.

A pack of race cars rumbled slowly around the track for the pace lap, with Flyer's red, white, and blue flagship car in the lead, behind the pace car.

Junker's and Specter's cars followed close behind Flyer. The cars all headed for the infield exit and left the racetrack. When they reached the parking lot, the cars drove slowly down a roped-off corridor through the sea of parked cars, heading for the interstate.

Junker activated his radio. "Specter," Junker called to his teammate. "We will be junking Team Fastex today, *ja?*"

Inside Specter's car, Stiles concentrated on driving, ignoring Junker's message.

"Specter?" Junker tried again. *"Ist du there? Ja?"*

The race cars approached the interstate onramp with their engines rumbling. Flyer's flagship car was still in the lead.

A red ribbon was stretched across the road.

At the top of the onramp, various officials and dignitaries, including Jack Fassler, watched from a bunting-draped grandstand. Because this race was cross-country, the spectators would only be able to see the start of it live. They'd catch the rest of the race on TV. SNIT planned to cover the whole event.

Vrrrrrrrrrooooooooommmmmmmm!

Flyer roared up the ramp and burst through the ribbon, snapping it.

The portable electronic flag board set up next to the grandstand flashed green.

Vrrrrrrrrrooooooooommmmmmmm!

Following Flyer's lead, the other cars roared past the grandstand, opening up their engines as they hit the newly paved interstate.

Mike Hauger and Pat Anther circled above the race in the SNIT chopper. As soon as the last car had whizzed underneath him, Mike took a deep breath. Then he announced, "And they're off!"

20

*S*cccccrrreeeeeeech!

Flyer's and Junker's cars banged together, swapping paint.

Junker worked his steering wheel furiously. "Your new paint job will be looking good on my car!" Junker screamed at Flyer. "Get me?"

Junker's and Flyer's cars both spun out, onto the shoulder of the interstate. The other cars passed them in a rush of hot wind. Stiles, in Specter's car, had taken the lead.

• • •

Inside the SNIT helicopter, high above the inter-state, Mike Hauger had just switched his coverage to a commercial. Mike leaned forward to where the pilot and cameraman were sitting. "Try to keep up with the lead car," Mike told the pilot.

Neither Pat nor Mike recognized the pilot—he was Forrest, one of the paramilitary guys who worked for Stiles! And the cameraman was Wilson!

Mike Hauger gave them a suspicious look. "You're new, aren't you?" he asked. "What happened to the regular crew?"

"They got tied up," Wilson replied.

Far below, a van was parked in the field behind the grandstand.

Inside the van were the real helicopter pilot and SNIT cameraman—gagged and bound with ropes. They struggled with the ropes and tried to yell for help, but Wilson and Forrest had done their work well.

Megan surged alongside Specter, starting to pass.

Stiles jerked the wheel towards Megan.

Bannnggg! Scccrrrreeeeeeeeeee! Their sides ground together for an earsplitting instant.

Suddenly, Stiles fired his booster rockets, sending both cars careening toward the shoulder of the road.

Megan's car spun out of control—right toward a lamppost!

She smashed through the lamppost, sending it flying end over end.

Stiles veered back onto the highway.

Unable to stop, Megan raced up a grassy hill and took off into the air.

21

*D*esperate to slow down, Megan threw her drogue chute lever.

She was headed right for the woods bordering the highway! The tree branches loomed dangerously over her windshield.

Floop!

Megan's drogue chute popped out of the back of her car and opened, slowing the car down.

But maybe she hadn't acted fast enough! Inch by inch, her car sailed through the air toward the thick woods. Megan fought the urge to cover her face with her hands. She needed to see what was going on, even if it meant getting poked in the face by a tree branch.

Finally, the drogue chute opened fully, and her car fell back to the ground.

Megan turned her car right before it crashed into the trees.

Quickly she headed back toward the interstate— she had a lot of catching up to do!

Inside the helicopter, Mike Hauger spoke to the camera. "We're seeing some real Unlimited action today!"

The helicopter was a couple of hundred feet up, following Specter's car.

Charger gained on Specter's car, and then blew past him to take the lead.

Inside Specter's car, Stiles reached for a lever on the dash marked GRAPPLING HOOK. He pulled it, and launched the hook. It crashed through Charger's rear window.

Ka-rraaaaaaashhhh!

The hook lodged in the dashboard next to Charger. "Hey!" he yelled as he spun out.

Stiles, in Specter's car, took the lead again.

Stunts zoomed by Charger, pursuing Specter's car. With every passing second, Stunts pulled a little closer. Finally, he found himself side by side with

Specter's car. Stunts got ready to pass. "You're not gonna run me off the road!" he swore.

Stiles threw a gas grenade out his window.

Stunts cried out as the grenade landed on the seat next to him.

"That's a grenade!" Stunts yelled in horror. He slammed on his brakes and skidded out.

Specter's car raced on ahead.

Wide-eyed, Stunts stared at the grenade beside him. He threw a lever on his control console. His jets fired, tipping the car up onto its passenger-side wheels. The grenade tumbled out the passenger window of the car—and burst into a cloud of gas.

Stunts's car fell back onto four wheels and spun off onto the shoulder of the highway, with the gas cloud harmlessly outside the car. "Why would a sneak like Specter cheat out in the open?" Stunts wondered. "It's like there's somebody else driving his car!"

Meanwhile, Flyer's car had breezed up behind Specter's car, gaining on it. Now it was Flyer's turn to try to pass.

Stiles swerved toward Flyer, his tires squealing.

Smmaaaaaaash!

They crashed together, grinding and scraping.

When the cars pulled apart, a broad swath of Flyer's new paint had been stripped away, revealing the colors underneath.

"Yellow and blue!" Stiles shouted.

Taking advantage of Stiles's loss of concentration, Flyer sprang past Specter's car.

Lyle Owens swept up behind Specter's car and moments later was passing it, too.

Stiles picked up a small handheld radio like the one Russell had used earlier. "The flagship car is the one we want!" Stiles announced over the radio. "Set up the ambush!"

22

On *Stiles's command, two bull-*
dozers rumbled into position side by side beneath
the overpass, their blades blocking the lanes used
by the racers.

The SNIT helicopter hovered above the overpass.
Mike Hauger peered out the chopper's window to
see what was going on. "It looks like there's some
sort of obstacle in the road," Mike reported.

Flyer's car roared around a turn.

"And here comes the race leader—Flyer Sharp in
the flagship car!" Mike announced.

As soon as Flyer got a good look at what was waiting for him under the overpass, his mouth dropped open in shock. "Roadblock!" he yelped. Flyer hurriedly threw a lever on his control console.

His wings flung out from the sides of his car, and his rocket boosters fired. Flyer jumped the overpass.

Up in the helicopter, Mike Hauger couldn't take his eyes off the wild action. "This race is really full of surprises," he told his audience.

Suddenly the helicopter swooped lower and Mike Hauger was pitched backward in his seat. Mike let out a short shriek.

The chopper swooped down toward Flyer's car, which had landed back on the highway once it cleared the overpass.

Mike Hauger and Pat Anther clung to their seats. "Good idea!" Mike Hauger said with terrified enthusiasm. "Go in for a closer shot!"

Wilson dropped his camera and pulled out a shoulder-fired rocket launcher.

"Is that a zoom lens?" Pat Anther asked. She gulped as the helicopter swooped down after Flyer's car.

Flyer's car whizzed down the interstate. "Attention all drivers!" Flyer shouted into his radio. "There are a couple of bulldozers blocking the road at the overpass! Repeat! The road is blocked!"

Lyle Owens laughed as he accelerated down the

highway, rounding the turn that led to the overpass. "Nice try, Flyer," he said, "but you don't expect me to believe some lame story about a—"

Lyle's eyes popped open wide as he saw the bull-dozers waiting under the overpass. "Roadblock!" he yelled. He desperately threw a lever on his control console. His rocket boosters fired as he tried to jump the overpass.

Lyle's car soared into the air . . . but he was too late.

Ka-rraaaaaaashhhh!

Impacting the hard metal overpass blew his car apart into a million pieces. Lyle's Rescue Racer zipped out of the wreckage, and skidded to a stop against the far guardrail of the overpass. The racer's canopy popped open, revealing a shell of impact foam. Owens, dazed, began chipping his way out of the quickly solidifying foam that had just saved his life.

Stiles rounded the bend and plowed across the median, engine roaring, crossing beneath the over-pass in the opposite lane. "Stop the flagship car!" Stiles hollered into his radio. "Don't let it get away!"

On Stiles's command, two monster trucks roared out of the woods and rumbled onto the highway ahead of Flyer.

Flyer's wheels screeched when he stomped on the gas. He fired his rocket boosters. Just as the two

monster trucks tried to ram him, Flyer launched ahead with a fiery burst of speed. The trucks swerved to follow.

Shhrrrreeeeeeeeeeeeeeeee!

The monster trucks sideswiped each other with a screech of twisted metal.

Inside the helicopter, Pat Anther watched carefully as Wilson aimed his rocket launcher. "See if you can zoom in on Steve 'Flyer' Sharp's face for a close-up!" Pat chirped.

Wilson squeezed the trigger.

Bfoom!

A missile whizzed toward Flyer's car.

With another screech, Flyer threw his car in reverse, backing up into a cloud of smoke created by his burnt tires. The rocket hit the ground right where Flyer had just been.

Ka-blaaammmmmmmm!

A fireball rose into the air, along with exploded chunks of asphalt.

Pat Anther looked horrified. "That's not a camera!" she hollered at Wilson. The chopper lurched violently and Pat toppled out of her seat. She screamed, panic and fear finally overtaking her.

On the interstate, Flyer kept zooming down the highway in reverse.

The two monster trucks scraped apart from each other and began to chase Flyer, gaining speed.

The helicopter swooped down again, heading toward Flyer.

Flyer gripped the wheel tighter, feeling full of determination. He did not know why the chopper and trucks were attacking him, but there was no way he was just going to sit there and take it. "The best defense is a good offense," he reminded himself. Then he stomped on the gas pedal and hit a lever on his control panel.

His rear wheels began to spin, squealing and smoking as they whirled faster in place. The second the wings of Flyer's car had stretched out to their full length, Flyer fired his booster rockets. His car launched into the air.

Wilson, up in the helicopter, had just been about to press the trigger of the rocket launcher. As Flyer took off, Wilson lowered the weapon slightly and turned to Forrest, the pilot. "Take it up!" Wilson ordered.

Airborne now, Flyer threw the grappling hook lever on his control console. The hook launched from Flyer's car, and sailed through the air. Flyer released the cord attached to the grappling hook as soon as it had cleared his launcher. The hook whizzed toward the chopper and clanged into the tail propeller.

Half the propeller broke off and spun away. The

remaining piece of propeller continued to whirl, tangling the grappling hook line around it.

Flyer's car landed safely and skidded to a halt.

The helicopter, without a tail propeller to control it, spun around wildly.

Mike Hauger and Pat Anther clung to each other in the back of the spinning chopper. Mike gathered his courage and spoke into his microphone. "This may be our final live broadcast," he informed his audience.

Pat Anther sat up straight. "But first," she chirped into her microphone, "a word from our sponsor!"

23

*T*he helicopter buzzed through the air, out of control, heading for a crash landing. Inside the copter, both Pat Anther and Mike Hauger screamed as the chopper came down in a field. Jolted by the rough landing, Mike and Pat's headsets—and their perfect hair—were knocked awry.

Stiles, still inside Specter's car, whipped over to Flyer's car and screeched to a stop alongside.

Flyer glanced over at the Team Rexcor car. He couldn't clearly see who was driving. "Specter," Flyer asked, "what's going on?"

Stiles pulled off his helmet. "You've got something that belongs to me!" he shouted. Then he tossed a gas grenade out his window. It sailed right through Flyer's open window, and burst. Flyer's car filled with a cloud of gas.

Before he knew it he was choking and coughing.

Meanwhile, Charger, Stunts, and a car from another team were rounding the bend that led to the overpass. Charger and the other team's car swerved away from Stunts. They bumped across the interstate median to avoid the bulldozers blocking the underpass, like Stiles had done earlier.

Stunts had a different plan. He fired his maneuvering jets, going up on two wheels at the last instant to slip through the space between the bulldozer blades. Sparks flew as Stunts's car scraped between the bulldozers.

On the other side of the underpass, Stiles jumped out of his car, and dropped down to his hands and knees beside Flyer's car. He reached under it, and pulled out the magnetic box with the component inside.

Vrrrrrrrrrooooooooommmmmmmm!

Stiles glanced up in alarm when he heard Stunts's car. It was heading right for him!

"Payback time, hombre!" Stunts yelled, his car dropping back onto all four wheels.

Stiles tucked the guidance component under his arm and ran for Specter's car. But Stunts rammed

Specter's car from behind before Stiles could jump back inside.

Stunts cleared his head by giving it a firm shake. Then he looked out at Stiles. "I knew it!" he said. "You're not Specter!"

Stiles turned around and ran.

Once again, Stunts fired his maneuvering jets in order to tip his car up onto two wheels. He roared after Stiles and zoomed around him, blocking his path like a wall.

Stiles paused as Stunts's car circled around him on two wheels.

"What's that you're trying to run off with, hombre?" Stunts called.

Suddenly a monster truck roared over and rammed Stunts's car. Stunts flipped over, his four wheels turning uselessly in the air.

Charger had gotten pretty far down the interstate, heading in the opposite direction before he glanced into his rearview mirror. His heart skipped a beat when he saw Stunts's car upside down. "What's going on, Carlos?" Charger asked over his radio. "You okay?" Without waiting for an answer, Charger spun in the road and raced back to help Stunts.

Inside his car, Stunts was dangling upside down in his harness. "I'm hanging in there," Stunts radioed back to Charger. "That guy driving Specter's car—I think he's the one who broke into our garage!"

Stiles jumped into a monster truck, which rumbled away down the interstate.

Rapidly changing course, Charger roared closer to the monster truck. "He's not getting away this time!" Charger vowed. He stopped short and then quickly threw a lever on his dash, launching his grappling hook.

24

*T*he grappling hook wrapped around the monster truck's axle. The wire cord connecting the axle to Charger's car pulled taut and slowly started towing Charger's car after the monster truck.

Stiles turned to the monster truck's driver. "Stomp on it!" he ordered. The driver smashed down the gas pedal and the engine roared. The truck's rear wheels spun and billowed out smoke.

Charger reached for the dash again, this time pulling a lever marked ROAD ANCHOR. The heavy, sharp anchor fell out the back of Charger's car, and dug deeply into the pavement.

The monster truck strained against the road anchor, its tires melting against the asphalt.

Suddenly the truck's rear axle yanked away, bouncing down the road. The bed of the truck banged down onto the asphalt.

After climbing out of the crashed helicopter, Wilson raised his rocket launcher to his shoulder and fired.

The rocket hit the front end of Charger's car.

Ka-blaaammmmmmmm!

The force of the explosion spun Charger's car around. Inside, Charger raised his hands in front of his face, shielding himself against the blast.

The front of Charger's car was a smoking ruin. Even before the smoke settled, Charger climbed out of the car.

"Let's get out of here!" Stiles shouted to Wilson and Forrest, who had both run up to join him on the road. Stiles took off running.

As Stiles dashed past Stunts's upside-down car, Stunts spotted his legs hurrying by. "Hey, hombre!" Stunts yelled. "Don't run off!" He reached for a lever on his dashboard, and his maneuvering jets fired.

With the blast of the jets, Stunts's car spun around on its crumpled roof. The fender bumped Stiles, knocking him off his feet.

Stiles hit the ground hard and cried out in pain. The guidance component flew out of his grasp and tumbled down the interstate. Suddenly, a grenade in Stiles's pocket burst, letting loose a cloud of gas that soon enveloped him.

Charger grabbed the guidance component off the ground. He looked up to see Wilson and Forrest escaping up a grassy slope to the overpass.

But just as Wilson and Forrest reached the road, two police cars, lights flashing and sirens blaring, skidded to a stop in front of them. Wilson and Forrest put up their hands.

Charger studied the guidance component.

Stunts freed himself from his car harness and hurried over to Charger. "What is this thing anyway?" he asked.

Charger handed the component to Stunts. "Property U.S. Government," he read off the side of the object. "Hey," Stunts said, "maybe there's a reward!"

Flyer groaned.

Stunts and Charger rushed over to Flyer's car and helped the semiconscious Flyer out of the vehicle.

"Keep going—" Flyer muttered groggily. "Pick up the flag—" Flyer fell back into unconsciousness as Charger and Stunts eased him down next to his car.

"He'll be all right," Stunts said. "But he won't be getting back in the race."

Vrrrrrrrrroooooooommmmmmm!

Charger and Stunts glanced up to see a group of

other team's cars roaring past on the opposite lanes of the interstate, continuing with the race. Junker, Zorina, and Megan zipped by. Charger stood up, staring at Flyer's car. "His car can still finish the race," he said.

Stunts nodded. "If one of us takes over as a relief driver, the championship points still go to the driver who started the race," he explained. "You want to help Flyer win the championship?"

"He'd do it for one of us," Charger replied.

Stunts glanced down at Flyer and grinned. "I'll stay with Flyer," Stunts told Charger. "You get charging!"

Charger ran over to Flyer's car and hopped inside.

Stunts squatted down beside Flyer. "Don't worry, soldier," he said, laying a reassuring hand on his unconscious teammate's shoulder. "Charger's gonna carry the flag for you."

His tires squealing, Charger headed down the highway in Flyer's car.

25

*S*ide by side, Junker and Zorina blasted down the Interstate.

Megan thrust her car between them, trying to pass. It didn't work. Megan threw Charger a desperate look as Junker's car swerved into her from one side.

Ka-runch!

Then Zorina's car swerved into her from the other side.

Ka-runch!

As Junker and Zorina veered out to gain momentum, Megan fired her turbojet boosters and roared forward, slipping in front of them. Junker and Zorina swerved in simultaneously to batter Megan, but crashed into each other instead.

Locked together by twisted metal, Junker and Zorina spun out and skidded down the interstate. Their terrified cries mingled as they crashed through an interstate exit sign and smashed into a fence before coming to a stop.

Junker and Zorina climbed out of their cars just in time to see Charger—in Flyer's flag-painted car—roar past them.

It didn't take long for Charger to catch up to Megan. He pulled up behind her, drafting. Together they hurtled toward the finish line.

With Charger on her tail, Megan passed under the electronic board and the checkered flag flashed.

Megan had won!

The Team Fastex hauler was parked in the training center parking lot near the personal cars of its drivers. Later that night, inside the hauler's locker room, Charger and Stunts got their overnight bags out of their lockers.

"I'm a driver, not a walking commercial," Charger told Stunts.

"You think your father and your grandfather never worked a supermarket opening?" Stunts asked. "You think being a McCutchen makes you too good for that?"

Charger slammed his locker shut and gave Stunts an annoyed look. "I'm not going to spend the off-season helping you sell autographed pictures!"

Megan walked up to them. She seemed serious, even irritated. "I need to talk to you," she told Charger. Then she glanced at Stunts. "Alone," she said.

Stunts shut his locker, overnight bag in hand. "Hey, *no hay problema,*" Stunts said. "There's a girl I promised to call, anyway. Come to think of it, there are about ten of them." He began walking away. "I better make it a conference call."

When Stunts was gone, Charger looked at Megan hopefully. "I've been hoping we could talk," he began. "Now that the season's almost over—"

"You let me win that race today, didn't you?" Megan asked, interrupting him. "You deliberately held back at the finish line instead of trying to pass me."

"I was driving Flyer's car," Charger protested.

Megan frowned angrily. "And the win would've counted for him?" she asked. "Is that it?"

"No," Charger replied. "That's not it! I'm just not used to his car! I was charging as hard as I could—"

"Don't lie to me, Mark!" Megan broke in. "And don't do me any favors. I can win my own races!"

With that, Megan turned and stalked angrily out of the locker room.

"Megan!" Charger called after her, but he didn't follow her. Shaking his head, he turned away, frustrated.

26

*I*nside the creepy Team Rexcor garage, squat, boxy repair robots rolled around on treads, using their multiple tool-ended arms to remove a battered body panel from a race car. Blue-flamed torches on the ends of the robot arms flared, and robot pincers peeled back the twisted metal.

"Two races left in the Unlimited Series," Garner Rexton growled, "and if Fastex wins just one of them, they win the team championship." He stood watching the repairs, the glow of the blowtorches reflecting in his eyes like fire burning inside him. "I'm not going to let Jack Fassler beat me."

Team Rexcor's robot crew chief, Spex, controlled the repair robots from a computer console near the battered car. Garner stood behind Spex, watching and brooding.

"Our cars and our drivers are a match for Fastex," Spex said in his mechanical voice. "We can win both races—"

"*Can* isn't good enough!" Garner exclaimed. "I *have* to win! I have to find a way to destroy Fastex."

A repair robot buzzed past Garner, carrying a spare part.

Garner kicked it.

The lights of Big River Raceway sparkled in the night sky.

A new experimental Unlimited Series racer—the Xpt–1—blazed out of a steeply banked turn.

Jack Fassler stood aboard the Team Fastex IMP in the pit area of the track. Near him was Megan, wearing a communications headset, and Duck, who was checking the car's performance with the computers built into the IMP. Miles hovered nearby, trying to peer over Duck's shoulder. Jack carefully watched the Xpt–1's progress along the track.

"The Xpt–1 is the best car we've ever built," Jack said.

Duck glanced up from the IMP's computer. "Even

the best car's only as good as the driver behind the wheel," he reminded Jack.

Inside the Xpt–1, Charger was driving. Out his window everything looked strangely fuzzy and blurry.

"You want me to check the compression again, Duck?" Miles asked. "I'll just punch it up on the computer—"

Duck nudged him out of the way with his thick body. "Don't touch that," he said.

Jack turned to his daughter and gave her a nod. "Okay, Megan," he said. "Go ahead with the test."

Megan pressed a button on her radio headset. "All systems are optimal, Charger," she announced. "Push the car to the outside of the envelope."

Inside the Xpt–1, Charger shifted into overdrive.

"Let's see what it can do," Megan said over the radio.

"Let's get charged!" Charger hollered.

Vvrrrrrrooooooooooommmmmmmm!

The engine roar increased as the car whipped around the track, way beyond the top speed of normal Unlimited Series racers.

Aboard the IMP, Jack smiled at Duck and Megan. "Congratulations," he told them. "The Xpt–1 is going to be the fastest thing on the track next season—"

"We got a problem here!" Charger interrupted over the radio.

Inside the Xpt–1, Charger struggled with the steering wheel. "I'm losing control!" he shouted.

Suddenly a wheel flew off the car. Tires squealing, the Xpt–1 spun out of control, flipped end over end, and exploded.

Miles's heart jumped in his chest. "Mark!" he screamed at his older brother.

27

Charger was thrown hard against his safety harness as the car flipped over and exploded. Flames blazed all around him. . . . Then the flames became fuzzier and vanished in a smear of computer graphics.

Charger pulled off his helmet.

Megan stepped over to his simulator cockpit. "What went wrong, Mark?" she asked.

"How are you supposed to race by remote control?" Charger shot back. He climbed out of the VR simulator, which had been set up in the pits, near the IMP where Megan, Jack, Duck, and Miles had been monitoring the test.

A few minutes later, Megan, Miles, Duck, and Jack picked through the wreckage of the remote-controlled car on the track. Flyer and Stunts put out lingering fires in pieces of wreckage with foam extinguishers. Charger, feeling disgusted, walked out onto the track.

Stunts whooshed his fire extinguisher at a piece of smoking wreckage, extinguishing it, and then looked up as Charger walked over to him. "You dinged this one up pretty good," Stunts teased.

"It wasn't my fault," Charger protested. "Something malfunctioned in the car."

Duck held up a piece of wreckage, examining it.

"Sure," Miles said to his older brother. "When Duck tries a new engine, it always blows up."

Duck tossed the piece of metal. It clanged on the track. He glanced at Miles. "Isn't it past your bedtime?" he asked Miles, sounding annoyed.

Charger turned to Jack and Megan. "Let me drive the other prototype, with none of this remote control stuff," Charger said. "If I'm really behind the wheel—"

"The Xpt–1 doesn't have a Rescue Racer built into it," Megan broke in. "If it crashes, you won't be able to escape."

Charger glared at her. "I'm not going to crash," he said stubbornly.

Jack stepped closer to them. "The kind of acceleration the Xpt–1 puts out may be more than any driver can handle," he explained.

Charger turned away, feeling frustrated. He kicked a small piece of wreckage, sending it clattering over the pavement.

"The Xpt–1 is still experimental, anyway," Jack continued. "We've got until next season to work the bugs out."

"If we don't win the team championship," Megan added, "Team Fastex may not be around for next season."

"We'll win," Jack said confidently. "All we have to do is beat Team Rexcor one more time."

The diner's neon sign glowed in the night.

"I'm on your tail, Flyer!" Stunts shouted.

Stunts and Flyer were in the diner's gaming room, both wearing VR goggles. They sat on opposite sides of an arcade game console called Jet Jockey. Charger stood nearby, watching them. Stunts and Flyer had their hands on the stick controls, lost in the fantasy of flying jet fighters. The game room echoed with the sounds of the game's air-to-air missiles firing and the whoosh of jet engines.

Suddenly Stunts sat up straight. "Hey, Flyer!" he shouted. "Where'd you go?"

Flyer's thumb was poised over the firing button on the stick controls of the arcade game. "Look behind you," Flyer said. His thumb pressed the button and the sound of missiles firing filled the room— followed by the sound of an explosion.

Stunts stared at the game controls in disbelief, as Flyer pulled off his VR goggles. Flyer got up and quickly left the game room.

Charger smiled at Stunts. "I guess the game's easier when you've flown real jets," he said.

In the main room of the diner, Megan was sitting at a table. Flyer walked over and sat down next to her. He wiped sweat from his face with a handkerchief.

"Are you okay?" Megan asked.

"That game reminded me of my last Air Force mission," Flyer explained, taking a deep breath. "It's nothing I can't handle."

Stunts and Charger came out of the game room and sat down at the table with Megan and Flyer.

"I would've won if I'd tried harder," Stunts claimed, "but I'm saving myself for the next race."

"What's so special about the next race?" Charger asked.

Megan smirked. "Do the math, Mark," she said. "We're all so close in points that one more win can give any one of us a lock on the individual driver's championship."

111

Charger raised his eyebrows at Stunts. "I guess I'll have to kick your bumper in the next race," he said. "Sorry."

"I'm planning on doing a little bumper-kicking myself," Flyer said.

Stunts grinned. "May the best man win," he said. "Me."

"You mean the best *person*," Megan added.

Suddenly, the sound of a door bursting open made the Team Fastex drivers turn around to look.

A big imposing man wearing sunglasses was standing in the diner's doorway. He looked like Arnold Schwarzenegger in *The Terminator*. Team Fastex's drivers glanced at each other as the man walked over to their table. His name was Kent Steele, but none of the Fastex drivers knew that.

"I hear NASCAR Unlimited Series drivers like to hang out here," Steele said. He had a dangerous, colorless voice.

"We're drivers," Flyer said. "The best."

"We're Team Fastex," Megan said, as if that explained everything.

"So, who are you?" Charger asked Steele.

Stunts grinned. "Charger," he asked, "don't you know a fan when you see one?" Stunts turned to face Steele. "Hey, hombre—you want my autograph?"

Slowly, Steele returned Stunts's grin—but his came out looking smug . . . and evil. "No," Steele said, and then stalked off to the game room.

Stunts and Charger exchanged glances, and then Stunts stood up. He walked over to where Steele was putting on a set of VR goggles for the Jet Jockey game.

"You want to play against another person," Stunts asked, "instead of against the computer?"

"It's all the same to me," Steele replied. He held out the second set of VR goggles, offering them to Stunts.

But Stunts shook his head. "I'm too good, man," he bragged. "It wouldn't be fair." He gestured with his hand toward Flyer, who was watching from the table. "But maybe Sharp here might be willing to take you on."

Flyer's hands shook as Stunts hurried back over to him.

Stunts bent down to whisper in Flyer's ear. "Teach this guy a lesson, Flyer," he murmured.

"You don't have to do this, Sharp," Megan said.

"Yes, I do," Flyer replied. He stood up abruptly, and strode over to the video game. He took the pair of VR goggles that Steele was offering and put them on.

The Jet Jockey game was only a little less realistic than the simulator Charger had used to test the Xpt–1. Flyer flexed his fingers, and then grasped the plane's stick, as the game console around him seemed to transform into a jet fighter cockpit. Flyer actually felt like he was soaring over a desert landscape.

But Flyer didn't have time to admire the view. Steele's fighter swooped in from the side, firing sizzling lasers. He missed.

Flyer banked his fighter and swerved around onto Steele's tail. He got ready to fire. "You only get one chance, rookie," Flyer said, "and you've had yours."

As Flyer fired at Steele's fighter, Steele suddenly put his plane through a wild, corkscrewing loop-the-loop.

Flyer chased him up into a cloud. When he came out, he was alone, with no sign of Steele's fighter. Flyer scanned the sky nervously. "This guy's good," he muttered.

Suddenly air-to-air missiles streaked past Flyer's fighter from behind.

"*Too* good!" Flyer yelped.

28

*S*teele's fighter zoomed over and got on Flyer's tail. Steele started firing.

Flyer banked and zigzagged desperately. Lasers whizzed past his fighter.

Cockpit alarms went off inside Flyer's cockpit. Flyer began to sweat and shake—he felt one of his nervous attacks coming on. He glanced behind him. "No!" he screamed.

Steele's fighter fired an air-to-air missile.

Flyer ejected from the cockpit as the air-to-air missile hit his plane and exploded.

Flyer pulled off his VR goggles. He was shaking and dripping with sweat.

Megan had come closer to watch the game. She leaned against Flyer, placing a comforting hand on his shoulder. "It's okay," she told him. "You're okay."

Charger and Stunts were staring at Flyer, amazed. "Man, you take these games too seriously," Stunts said.

Charger looked at Flyer, worried. "There's something wrong with him," he said.

Steele got up from his seat at the game console and confronted the four Team Fastex drivers. "Maybe he doesn't have what it takes," he growled.

Charger stepped up to Steele, so close their noses were almost touching. "Hey, leave him alone!" Charger said. "He's just feeling sick or something—"

Steele grabbed Charger's shirt, lifting him off the ground. "Maybe you don't have what it takes, either," he snarled.

Charger grabbed Steele's arm, struggling to loosen his hold, but Steele tossed him effortlessly across the room. Charger crashed into a table, breaking it.

Stunts jumped in front of Steele, getting into his face. "I've got what it takes," Stunts threatened,

"and you're about to get it!" Stunts threw a punch at Steele.

But Steele caught Stunts's hand before impact, his reflexes incredibly fast.

Stunts's eyes widened in surprise.

Steele smiled smugly—and then shoved Stunts backward. Stunts flew across the room and crashed into the wall beside the broken table. Steele started walking menacingly toward the fallen Charger and Stunts.

Flyer lunged over and grabbed Steele. "The fight's over!" he yelled.

Steele shrugged Flyer off, sending him flying across the room. Flyer crashed into the wall beside Charger and Stunts. Steele continued forward toward Charger, Stunts, and Flyer.

Megan jumped in Steele's way. "Stop it!" she ordered. She glanced back at Charger, Stunts, and Flyer. "All of you!"

Steele stopped, looking down at Megan with a sneer on his lips. "I guess drivers don't have to be tough," he said with a nasty laugh. "It's the car that does all the work." With an evil smile, he turned and stomped out of the game room.

When Steele was gone, Stunts, Charger, and Flyer began to pick themselves up off the floor.

"Good thing for him he left," Stunts said groggily. "I was about to put him in need of major body work."

Megan gazed thoughtfully after Steele. "Whoever he is," Megan said, "I just hope we never run into him again."

Gloom seemed to ooze from the corners of Garner Rexton's office in the Rexcor headquarters building. "Team Rexcor must win the next race to keep Team Fastex from taking the Unlimited Series team championship," Garner told Lyle Owens. He stared at Lyle across his huge desk. "Are you willing to do what it takes to help this team win?" Garner asked.

"Whatever it takes, Mr. Rexton," Lyle replied quickly.

Garner got up from behind his desk. "I'm glad to hear it," he said. "Because to make sure that Team Rexcor wins . . . I'm replacing you with a new driver."

Lyle stared at his boss in total shock. "But, but . . . you can't do that!" he spluttered. "I'm the best you've got, Mr. Rexton! I'm The Collector!"

Garner didn't reply. He was busy gazing out the window of his office.

"I'm—" Lyle began. "I'm—"

"Unemployed?" Garner supplied.

Lyle shook his head, trying to make sense of what his boss was saying. Then he got up and walked over to Garner, who was still staring out the win-

dow. "Mr. Rexton," Lyle said, "a new driver won't have the experience to handle Team Fastex."

Garner looked at Lyle and smiled. "This driver can do anything Team Fastex can do," he said. He walked past Lyle and opened the door to his office. "This meeting is over," he said.

For a moment Lyle looked puzzled and hurt. Then he narrowed his eyes and stalked out of Garner Rexton's office.

29

*T*he *Rexcor Raceway buzzed with* activity. The parking lots were full to capacity, and the Fizz Cola blimp circled overhead.

Standing in front of a huge crowd of excited fans, with Pat Anther at his side, Mike Hauger spoke into his microphone. "Today's race could decide the winner of the first NASCAR Unlimited Series team championship!" he exclaimed. Mike and Pat both smiled into the camera. "If Team Fastex wins today," Mike continued, "the championship is theirs."

Pat smiled again, showing all of her big white

teeth. "And it's not just the team championship at stake for Team Fastex, Mike. If any one of Jack Fassler's drivers wins today, he or she will have an almost unbeatable lead in the race for the individual driver's championship."

The Team Fastex drivers walked out of their hauler one by one. They all looked very serious, mentally preparing themselves for the big race. They wandered over to the pits, where they watched Duck working on a car with a whining torque wrench.

"Does anybody know this rookie driver for Team Rexcor?" Jack asked. "His name's Kent Steele."

"He might as well park it now, man," Stunts said. "If he's never driven a NASCAR Unlimited Series race, he'll be a pushover!"

Megan glanced at the guys. "It's time for the drivers' meeting," she said.

Charger turned and headed toward the drivers' meeting room. Megan hurried to catch up with him. To get to the room, they had to walk underneath a vine-covered trellis arching over a walkway. On the trellis was a sign on it that read THROUGH THIS GATE PASS THE BEST DRIVERS IN THE WORLD.

Charger hurried under the trellis, leaving Megan behind.

"Mark!" Megan called. "Wait."

Charger stopped to wait for Megan. The meeting room's door was right next to Charger. It was just a

plain portable building with DRIVERS ONLY written above the door.

Megan took a deep breath once she'd reached Charger. "What I said the other day about not doing me any favors—"

"I didn't let you win, Megan!" Charger interrupted.

"How can I be sure?" she asked, starting to get angry. "That's why I can't let anything happen between us! Friends can compete against each other, but if other feelings get involved, it messes everything up!"

Charger took a step closer to her until they were almost touching. "Then you do have feelings for me," he said.

Megan groaned in frustration. Turning on her heel, she stormed inside the meeting room.

Stunts and Flyer walked through the trellis behind Charger, heading for the meeting room. "If you two are arguing about who's going to win the championship," Stunts told Charger, "you can save your breath. I'm going to be the individual driving champion. No question about it!"

"I might have something to say about that," Flyer put in.

"It's going to take more than talking to beat me," Charger added. He turned and started to walk toward the meeting room.

"You think they have some leftover trophies with *McCutchen* on them?" Stunts called after him.

A look of anger crossed Charger's face. He turned around to confront Stunts.

Stunts grinned. "Or maybe your grandfather's ghost is going to come back and drive the car for you!" he taunted Charger.

"I've heard enough outta you!" Charger shouted.

Flyer stepped between them, trying to keep them from fighting. "All right!" he said. "Break it up!"

Stunts glared at Flyer. "If you wanted to give orders, you should've stayed in the Air Force!"

"From now on," Charger exclaimed, "it's every man for himself!"

"Team Fastex," came a familiar, sarcastic voice from behind them.

The three drivers whirled around to see who was speaking.

Kent Steele was standing under the trellis in a Team Rexcor driving suit. He smiled his smug, evil smile. "Showing your team spirit?" he asked.

Charger, Flyer, and Stunts stared in surprise as Steele pushed past them.

Zorina followed Steele past the Team Fastex guys. "How do you like Rexcor's new driver, baby?" she asked.

The three Team Fastex drivers stared after Steele. They had nothing more to say.

30

*O*n the Rexcor Raceway track, the cars began their warm-up lap before the start of the race.

Jack and Duck stood at the pit wall, watching as cars rumbled past. Duck raised a handheld radio to his mouth. "I want you to keep each other posted on this new guy—Kent Steele," he instructed the Fastex drivers. "Team Rexcor may be up to something, so watch each other's bumpers."

"You guys are going to be in a good place to watch my bumper," Stunts called to his teammates over the radio. "Behind me."

"We're here to compete," Charger told Duck over the radio. "Not help each other."

The electronic board flashed the green flag.

Vrroooooooommmmmmmmmmm!

The ranks of Unlimited Series cars plunged across the starting line.

In the Team Rexcor hauler's communications room, Garner Rexton watched a bank of TV monitors showing the cars gushing down the track. Garner raised a microphone. "You know what to do, Steele," he told his newest driver over his communications system. "Your only reason for existing is to beat Team Fastex."

In his car, Steele smiled his chilling smile as he wove in between the racing vehicles surrounding him.

"My only reason for existing is to beat Team Fastex," he repeated coldly.

Up in the Rexcor Raceway broadcast booth, Pat Anther and Mike Hauger were reporting on the race. "Mike," Pat said into her microphone, "before the race I had the chance to talk to the drivers about winning the drivers' championship." A large screen descended behind her. "Let's hear what they had to say," Pat continued.

Megan appeared in close-up on the screen. "My parents have always encouraged me to demand more from myself," she said.

On the track, Megan swerved around Zorina's car and fired her side-mounted boosters to zoom past her.

On the screen, Megan was still talking. "Winning the championship is the greatest challenge of all," she continued. "For the cars I've helped to build, but most of all, for myself."

Megan's image on the screen behind Pat Anther faded. Now Stunts appeared on the screen. "My family isn't famous or rich," Stunts said, "but they're real champions."

In the race, Stunts's car pushed up fast behind two cars from other teams. He fired his maneuvering jets and tilted up on two wheels to slip between the slower cars, passing them.

"I'm going to bring it all home for them: the championship, the fame, the money," Stunts said on Pat Anther's screen. "*La vida buena*—the good life they deserved but never had."

Next up on Pat's screen was an interview with Flyer. "A soldier going into combat is afraid, but he keeps going, despite that fear inside him," Flyer said.

Down on the hot asphalt of Rexcor Raceway, Flyer was trapped behind Specter's car. He extended his wings and fired his turbojet booster to jump over Specter.

"Victory is the proof that he was stronger than his fear," Flyer continued on Pat's screen. "Winning the driver's championship means that I kept going."

Now it was Charger's turn to appear in Pat Anther's taped video interview. "My father and grandfather are gone," Charger said. "I can't bring them back."

On the track, Charger's car came out of a high-banked turn and swung around a car from another team.

"But as long as I do what they would've done," Charger continued in the video, "it's like somehow they're still here."

Charger pulled alongside Junker's car on a straightaway. Junker swerved toward Charger, trying to smash into him—Junker's typical method of dirty driving. Charger threw a lever on his control console to fire his boosters. He accelerated out of the path of Junker's attack.

Junker missed him. He crashed into the wall, bounced off, and spun out.

Stunts and Steele raced down the track toward Junker's spinning car. They both fired their maneuvering jets and tilted up onto two wheels. Stunts and Steele roared past, both on two wheels, on opposite sides of Junker's car.

As his car flopped back onto four wheels, Stunts glanced toward Steele's car. "This guy's been learning from the best," he said. "Me!"

Steele's car swung around Stunts, his engine roaring.

Megan spurted up behind Stunts. "I've never seen anybody run as fast as Steele!" Megan said to her teammates over her radio. "We'll have to draft together just to stay up with him!"

Stunts scowled. "I'm not going to win the championship riding Steele's bumper!" he replied hotly to Megan. Stunts pulled away from Megan's car and roared up beside Steele, trying to pass on the low side of the track.

Steele peered without expression over at Stunts's car, and then abruptly turned his wheel.

Baaaang!

Steele's car smacked into Stunts.

"Try it again, rookie!" Stunts taunted Steele.

Steele smiled at the wheel. "Stunts will try the other side this time," he muttered to himself.

Stunts began to catch up to Steele, but then suddenly swerved to try to pass on the opposite side, between Steele and the wall.

Steele veered toward the wall, whacking into Stunts.

Speeding out of control, Stunts crashed against the wall. Immediately, his car filled with quick-hardening impact foam.

In the Team Rexcor hauler, Garner smiled grimly as he watched the race on the monitors. "That's one down," he said.

31

*S*teele's car hurtled down the track.

Mike Hauger sat up straight in his broadcast booth chair. "This is incredible!" he shouted. "Rookie driver Kent Steele is posting the fastest times ever in a NASCAR Unlimited Series race!"

Steele wove around three cars in a staggered line, passing them as smoothly as if they were cones on an obstacle course.

"Pat," Mike Hauger asked his co-anchor, "just who is this phenomenal rookie driver who seems to have come out of nowhere?"

"According to Steele's bio," Pat replied, "team owner Garner Rexton found him on the assembly line at a Rexcor Corporation factory."

"From assembly line worker to race car driver," Mike said self-importantly. "Truly an inspiring story."

Meanwhile, back in the race, Steele scrambled to pass Flyer, who was running low on the track.

Jack and Duck twisted their heads as the cars zoomed by pit wall. Jack raised a handheld radio. "Charger, move down by Flyer and block Steele out!" he instructed.

"I'm in the groove, Jack!" Charger replied over his radio. "Moving down would only slow me up!"

Flyer struggled for position, trying to block Steele on his own. "I don't need Charger's help!" Flyer told Jack.

But no sooner had Flyer spoken than Steele roared past him.

Steele reached calmly for a lever on his dashboard at the same time as Flyer did the same thing inside his own car.

They fired their turbojet boosters simultaneously, and both cars jumped into the air, with Steele in front of Flyer.

"Look out!" Flyer hollered. He had to yank his wheel hard to avoid smashing into Steele in midair. Flyer's car made a crash landing and blazed into the infield, plowing up the turf.

Steele's car landed safely on the track. He smiled in satisfaction.

Inside the Rexcor hauler communications room, Garner was smiling, too. "Two down and two to go," he said. "McCutchen next."

A slower car bumped Charger as he passed it, and suddenly Steele's car whizzed through the slot, passing both of them. Charger gushed up after Steele, drafting behind him to avoid wind resistance on his car.

Megan roared up behind Charger.

Charger contacted Megan over the radio. "I'm passing Steele when we come out of the next turn!" he told her.

"He's too fast!" Megan argued. "We should draft for a few more laps before we make our move!"

Charger wiped sweat from his face and clutched the steering wheel, shaking his head. "I'm not like Stunts and Flyer!" he said. "I can handle Steele!"

Charger swept up alongside Steele's car. He threw the lever for his booster rockets.

Steele remained perfectly calm. "Now," he said. He swerved hard toward Charger as Charger's booster rockets started to fire. Steele crunched into him, jamming his rockets shut.

Blaaaaaammmmmm!

The jammed booster rockets blew off a big chunk of Charger's car.

With his car wrecked and smoking, Charger spun

out of control and crashed into the track wall.

Megan's eyes widened as she desperately tried to steer her car past the wreck. She couldn't help side-swiping Charger's wrecked car. Her car tumbled into the air, turning on its side.

It smashed down hard, throwing sparks as it slid along the pavement to a stop.

Steele kept driving as if nothing had happened. His smile turned into a grin.

Charger climbed out of his ruined car. When he spotted Megan's wrecked car, his stomach twisted painfully. "Megan!" he screamed, rushing over to her.

Megan began to pull herself out of her crumpled racer. She was crying, wiping tears angrily from her eyes.

In a second, Charger stood beside her. "Are you all right, Megan?" he asked. His voice was thick with caring and worry.

Megan shook her head. "We could've won the team championship today," she said angrily, "but we didn't!" She pushed past Charger and stormed away.

"If it wasn't for that guy Steele—" Charger began.

Megan glanced back at him, cutting off his words. "It's *our* fault!" she told him firmly. Megan started to walk again, leaving Charger gazing after her helplessly.

The checkered flag on the electronic board flashed as Steele's car roared across the finish line.

"Kent Steele has done it!" Mike Hauger cheered.

"Imagine how excited he must be," Pat Anther said, "after winning his first NASCAR Unlimited Series race!"

Just past the finish line, Steele sat at the wheel. He stared straight ahead, with no emotion on his face.

He did not even blink.

32

*I*n the pits a little while later, Jack glared at the four Team Fastex drivers who were standing beside Flyer's battered car.

The drivers all looked awful—Stunts's arm was in a sling; Flyer had a bandage on his head; Charger's driving suit was torn and scorched; Megan's suit was ripped and her face was smeared with grease and dirt. Duck and Miles looked on nervously.

Jack cleared his throat. "I didn't see Team Fastex out on that track today!" he yelled at Stunts, Flyer, Charger, and Megan. "All I saw was four drivers out for their own personal glory!"

Stunts stepped forward. "We would've won, if it wasn't for Steele!" he protested.

"It's like he knows everything we do before we do it!" Flyer added.

"Don't be too hard on them, Jack," Garner Rexton said.

Jack turned, his eyes widening in surprise as Garner walked over to the group.

"Your drivers did the best they could," Garner said. "They're only human."

"Did you come down here to gloat, Garner?" Jack asked.

Garner pretended to be offended. "No, Jack," he said. "I came over to wish you luck. We're tied for the team championship now." He tried to hide the hint of an evil smile that played on his lips. "May the best man win," Garner said.

That night, a pool of harsh light shone in the otherwise dark Team Rexcor garage. In the spotlight, Steele sat on a crate near his car. Spex stood behind him.

Garner paced back and forth in front of Steele. "The team that wins the next race will win the team championship," Garner reminded them. "The last race—all or nothing."

Spex popped out a torque wrench from his arm

and touched the whirring tool to something hidden in Steele's hair.

Steele suddenly began talking. "My only reason for existing is to beat Team Fastex—" he began. Then he froze in the middle of his speech.

Spex lifted off Steele's face and the top of his head, removing a lifelike mask to reveal a gleaming metal robotic skull. A cranium packed with circuits and wires glittered in the dark garage.

Steele was an android!

"Steele is programmed with the combined skills of all the Team Fastex drivers," Spex said in his mechanical voice, "downloaded from their own simulator. He can't lose."

"I want him to do more than just win," Garner told Spex. He bent down to peer at Steele's creepy skull-like robotic face. "I want him to destroy Team Fastex."

With a faint whine of electric motors, Steele's metallic facial gears moved, revealing more of his human-looking teeth.

Once again, Steele smiled his smug, evil, chilling smile.